THE DAY BEFORE TOMORROW

DAVID HELWIG

For Bill Barnes, Dennis Crossfield and Harvey Shepherd

How else, at this moment of history, can one behave except badly?

Guy Burgess

1

The quiet was gone now, and he wished the city again empty and silent as in those first minutes when he moved in peace along the unknown streets, but more and more cars rushed past him while more people joined the queues waiting for the high red buses or walked in silent concentration into the tube stations and hurried downward to the trains. There was a sudden rush to bring London to life, thousands of bodies wakened and forced out into the chilly morning to repeat the pattern of all their days.

He no longer moved in his pattern. He walked at random, unable to think where he should go, waiting.

He saw himself reflected in a shop window, a small round-faced man. He still wore his dark, three-piece suit, but the trousers were wrinkled now.

From street to street he went on, turning suddenly now and then to see if he was being followed. Each time he turned, he searched the streets and found no-one he could suspect. And was surprised. He was almost disappointed, but he knew they might still be there somewhere, just out of sight. He hardly cared now. He would simply wait for what was to come.

He wondered where he was. Somewhere south of the river still, for he had crossed no bridge, though he thought that he was moving north.

He remembered a story he had read when he was a child, about a trapper lost in the forest somewhere in Northern Ontario. It was snowing in the story and getting dark, and the man had somehow lost his bearings. The trapper had been afraid that he was walking north into the bush and would never find help. He had forgotten the ending of the story.

The landscape here was as anonymous and hostile as that forest, blocks of flats that all looked the same, closed circles of acquaintanceship.

He still had ten or fifteen pounds in his wallet. Perhaps soon he'd stop and eat. Many of the stores around him were closed, their windows covered with corrugated iron. They were the neighbourhood shops for the old terrace houses that had been pulled down to make way for the new flats, though here and there a terrace survived, sometimes boarded up, sometimes still in use.

There was a restaurant beside him with windows steamed up from the heat and fumes of cooking. He walked in. The small room was filled with square tables and straight-backed chairs. A couple of workmen were having breakfast.

He walked to the counter at the back, got an egg and sausages and a cup of tea. As the woman poured the tea from a pitcher it slopped over the edge of the cup.

He carried the food to a table where he put down the tray. He drank some of the tea. It was strong and tasted metallic, but the warmth pleased him. He tried to eat, but found that he didn't want the food now that he had it.

An old woman came in the door. She walked slowly across to the counter where she got a cup of tea. There were empty tables all around, but she brought her tea across to his table where she sat down opposite him. He glanced at her and then looked back down at his food. He thought she looked familiar, but he couldn't think where he had seen her.

His eyes flickered up and found that she was staring

at him. He wondered if she could be some kind of messenger, but she said nothing, gave no sign of recognition, only stared. He drank more of his tea and ate a few bites of egg. The woman drank her tea noisily.

He got up to leave, unable to eat more, afraid now that the woman would follow him or shout after him, but once he had got up from the table she ignored him. When he glanced back, she was concentrating on her tea.

When he reached the street again, he started to walk automatically, the same way he had been walking before, as if he had some distant goal to reach. He still thought a message of some sort might come, telling him where he should go, though he wasn't sure that if a messenger came he wouldn't run from him in order to resume this random walking. He was becoming wholly involved in it, step after step, just the exact right speed, moving forward, seeing little of what he passed by, like the old men in seedy overcoats who slept in the streets and parks.

Perhaps he would become like that. It had its fascination.

Once or twice as he walked, he tried to call himself back, to think clearly as he had the night before, but he could only grasp images, and each image seemed to have its own particular pain and terror.

He would have to write something if he wanted to think more clearly, but he wasn't sure he did want that. He only wanted to walk steadily in one direction. It was very satisfying.

He found himself wondering about the passage of time. His feet moved steadily forward as he went along the grey pavement, and the movement of his feet seemed like the measuring of time in a grey emptiness. As if he could become time by moving so steadily, pace by pace, watching only the movement of his feet.

In front of him he noticed a man staring in the window of a store. It was a book store, and the window was full of sex books with badly-drawn pictures on the front.

He walked into the store. It was crowded with piles of books, which made it hard to move from place to place. There were two clerks, both Pakistanis, and a couple of men stood around leafing through the books. There were piles of almost identical books with the same bright yellow colours and bad drawings. He picked up one called *Strange Desires*. On the front was a picture of a naked woman cowering before a man with high leather boots and a whip. He put the book back down and turned toward the door of the shop. He could see over the top of the racks in the windows and saw there the faces of two men staring at the racks of books. Their eyes did not move.

He walked out of the shop and down the street again. The books had drawn him away from concentration on his walking and made him think backward and forward, brought memories and plans into his head. He felt panic and almost began to run, but by walking on, just walking steadily on, he calmed himself.

2

There had been faces, many faces all around, turning toward him, demanding. He had betrayed. Or might. The heavy faces had insisted on that and bayonets were held at him. But he had awakened before they killed him. That was the important thing. Over the years Jake had always known that the one moment he mustn't allow to happen in a dream was the moment of his own death. If he died in a nightmare, he would never wake or would wake crazy.

Jake rolled over and opened his eyes for a moment; the blue walls of his room looked almost clean in the bright sunlight. It had been a bad night, more nightmare than sleep. He wondered if he had been screaming. Sometimes he would scream in his sleep. For years, since he was a child, Jake had slept badly, haunted by his dreams. Sometimes he was almost afraid to go to sleep for fear of what might come.

And last night in his dream, the revolution had come, and Jake had been one of the casualties.

Revolution, revolution, revolution. It seemed to Jake sometimes that even to use the word was to confront his own violent nightmares and defeat them. To feel that fire and death were part of wisdom. Yet when he approached violence in life, his mind hid back in itself, fled. A few months before he'd seen a car accident, and he still remembered a man lying on the pavement with a blood stain on his shirt and another behind his head.

That was only one man, an accident, but perhaps it was worse because it was an accident, meaningless. Jake remembered being in a bar one night during the Democratic Convention. Everyone in the room was staring at the television set, entranced, watching people running and being hit, and finally as a cop was seen beating his stick on a kid's back, a man in the room stood up, his eyes reaching out toward the television set, and shouted "Give it to the fucker. Kill him."

Nightmares. Revolutions. He thought about the argument with Member and reached for his little red notebook from the table beside the bed. When he got back last night he'd written a few lines of poetry in it. He turned to the page.

13

> The man looked up
> at me and said
> Does the death train stop
> near here, my friend?
>
> And I looked down
> at him and said
> It passed you by
> last night my friend.

He'd been annoyed and depressed by the argument, but at least when he fought with Member the argument meant something because they understood each other, spoke the same language.

Jake remembered where the faces came from, the faces in his dreams. They were the faces of the peasant militia in a poster that Member had on his wall. In the poster they were beautiful faces, but the way the group of them thrust foward was threatening. The people militant. The people armed.

What happened when your nightmares became real? Jake wished he could talk to someone who had been in Chicago. Probably when the police came for you everything was simple. And afterwards? Did you need to be attacked again and again?

Jake picked up a magazine from beside the bed and looked for a sentence he'd noticed last night. He read it again. *Revolutionaries are interested in politics, not personal salvation; they are interested in changing society, not merely in defying it.* He had underlined the sentence with his ball point and now he tore out the page of the magazine. That was close to what he'd been trying to say to Member last night.

The Action Group had voted to hold a sit-in at the City Council chambers and one at the administration offices at the same time. Jake had never got clear in his mind exactly what was to be proved by this, though Member, who'd initiated the idea, kept talking about complicity, and apparently they were going to prove this by getting thrown out of both places the same day. They didn't have a clear issue or any kind of long-term plan. It was just a gesture. There had been a lot of talk about housing problems everywhere in Canada, and in Kingston, discussion of students putting people out of their places by crowding in and paying higher rents, but they hadn't got the situation defined to the point where they could make an effective demonstration. At least that was how it seemed to Jake, but Member and a lot of the others were convinced that what really mattered was to keep attacking, just keep demonstrating and picking up recruits until someone in authority made a stupid mistake. After that it was simple. He remembered something that Member had said the night before.

"It's the only clean thing to do," he'd shouted at Jake.

Jake really must show him that quotation. Not that it would convince him, but Jake wanted to make the point. He knew that he'd go along with the demonstration if it was held. The group had voted and he'd go with them. Get thrown in jail if he had to, but he'd like to have been a bit more sure what they were supposed to be gaining. He wanted to feel that they were hitting where it would hurt. Still, it would be good to see Member in action again, that round face shining with excitement, his chubby hands pushing the curly black hair back from his face.

Jake got out of bed and wandered around the room in his underwear looking for food. There wasn't much, but he had a glass of orange juice and some cookies. As he ate, he stood at the back window and looked out into the bright autumn sunlight. It would be a good day to go out in the country, and Jake wished he had a car. He supposed he could borrow Member's.

There was a light knock at the door, and Willy walked in. She lived with a law student in a room

15

upstairs. After he left in the morning, she liked to come down and get into bed with Jake.

Willy closed the door behind her. She was wearing a long sweater that just managed to cover her behind.

"Hi," she said. She took off the sweater and climbed into his bed.

"God, you're skinny," she said.

"Yes," Jake said, "I am. Always have been."

"Know what?" she said. "Doug wants to get married, like right away, as soon as we can get the licence and everything. I might marry him too, cause I've always wanted to be a divorcée."

Jake ate another cookie.

"You're so goddam skinny and silent," she said. "I never know what to make of you."

Jake finished his cookie.

"Look," she said, "are you going to fuck or shall I go somewhere else?"

"Be patient," Jake said.

He took off his underwear and got into the narrow bed with her. She was slim and strong and tense.

"C'mon, you skinny bastard," she said, "work."

Jake worked hard for her, and afterwards he was tired and felt like sleeping. The pain in his stomach had come back, but Willy wasn't ready to let him doze off. She began to stimulate him with her hands and her long fingernails, and it occurred to him what vicious little hands they could be.

Someone knocked at the door. Jake was slow to react, and Willy answered first.

"Who's there?" she said in a sweet little-girl voice.

"I'm looking for Jacob Martens."

"Just a second," Jake said and got out of bed. He pulled on his jeans and went to the door. The man at the door was big. He wore a plaid sports jacket and a tie that didn't match.

16

"I'm Sergeant Talbot," he said. "RCMP."

Jake remembered that they always came in groups to bust people, and he didn't think they always knocked at the door.

"I'd like to talk to you," the man said.

"Sure," Jake said.

The man walked into the room. Willy looked at him and gave him a big smile. He nodded. There was only one chair in the room, and it was covered with clothes and magazines. Jake pushed them onto the floor.

"Have a seat," he said.

The more he thought about it, the less it looked like a drug bust. It must be something else, maybe a warning about his political activities.

"I believe you have a brother named John Martens in the Department of External Affairs."

"Is that true, Jake?" Willy said. "I didn't know you had a brother."

Jake noticed that she was letting the covers slip off her because she thought the horseman wasn't paying enough attention. The man glanced at her and back at Jake.

"Willy," Jake said, "why don't you go upstairs, and I'll see you later."

"You're a shit, Jake," she said. She threw back the covers, put on her sweater and walked out. The mountie was still trying not to look. After she closed the door, Jake turned back to him again.

"John Martens is your brother?"

Jake nodded.

"Have you heard from him recently?"

"I got a letter from him a month or two ago."

"Did he say anything unusual?"

"Why? What's this all about?"

"I've been asked to inform you that your brother has disappeared in England under suspicious circumstances. The authorities there believe he's been involved in espionage. If he's found, he'll be prosecuted."

17

"That's impossible," Jake said. "He's the straightest guy I've ever met, I mean he's really straight. What kind of evidence do they have?"

"I'm sorry, I'm not allowed to tell you that."

"I think it sounds phoney. Where's he gone?"

"No-one knows. The English police are looking for him. If they find him he'll be prosecuted. If he should happen to get in touch with you, we'd appreciate it if you'd let us know."

"I suppose he's going to phone me transatlantic to say where he's hiding out."

"He might try to come back to Canada."

"Who was he spying for?"

"I'm not allowed to tell you that."

"Jesus Christ," Jake said.

The mountie took out a notebook.

"I'll leave you my telephone number," he said.

"In case there are any more questions I want not answered."

"In case your brother should get in touch with you."

"You don't really think I'd call you."

"I'd advise you to. This is a serious matter."

"Have you told my old lady?"

"I think someone will be in touch with her."

"She's going to be awfully confused. She's not, like, very political."

The mountie handed Jake the slip of paper with his name and phone number on.

"Did your brother ever say anything that would have made you suspect this?" he said.

"I haven't seen him for maybe two years. I used to get letters now and then, but he always sounded really stuffy. Do you think I'm in on a big communist plot?"

"I didn't say that, did I?"

The mountie walked to the door.

"You'll be here if we need to contact you again?"

"I guess so."

The big man took the sports jacket and unmatching tie out the door.

"Jesus Christ," Jake said out loud and sat down in the empty chair. He tried to remember John, the last time he'd seen him, when he came home for a short visit before going to England. All he could really remember was the round puffy face, clean shaven, with horn-rimmed glasses; that and the three-piece suit that made him look formal and old fashioned. Jake remembered too the slow careful patterns of speech, with a little pause at the end of each sentence. And whenever he remembered John, he remembered Margaret beside him, not speaking much and stammering when she did, a kindly distant woman, just a sort of presence, like some kind of ghost following his brother, haunting him.

He tried to imagine his brother as a spy, but he couldn't make the thing fit. Would he do it for money? It didn't seem likely, in fact it seemed impossible. John wasn't greedy; he'd paid Jake's university fees for the last four years.

Two years before Jake finished high school, John had written to him saying that he and Margaret would be happy to pay the fees if Jake could look after the rest of his expenses. Jake had felt guilty about accepting, but it had saved him going into debt.

Jake was embarrassed to remember the letters he had sent his brother over the last few months, cocky, hectoring letters in which he used his brother's supposed liberalism as a stalking horse, sometimes trying out arguments he didn't entirely accept to shock John or see where the idea led. His attitude to John had always been a bit patronizing, at least since he'd been old enough to have real opinions, for there was something almost comical about the man, something pedantic and precise and foolish.

He tried to create a picture in his mind of John

19

at a secret meeting in some dark corner of a restaurant, but what came to his mind was a picture of his brother delivering a rather pompous little lecture to his contact on how they ought to be organizing things.

It was like hearing that Willy had become a nun, no, even more unlikely than that, for Willy would do anything that anyone said she couldn't or shouldn't.

Jake wandered around the room, put on his clothes and picked up some of the mess from the floor. He had a class at eleven, but he didn't feel much like going. He decided to walk over to Member's place and see if he could borrow the car. When he got outside, it was bright and warm in the sun. He walked quickly over to Member's, hoping that he'd be there and would let Jake take the car, or that both of them could go out into the country in it.

Jake went up the dark stairway two steps at a time and pounded on the door. He'd seen the car parked outside, so Member was likely here, probably still asleep. Jake pounded on the door a couple more times, and finally there was a bit of noise inside, and Member appeared at the door with a towel wrapped around his fat hairy body.

"What's with the towel?" Jake said. "You becoming respectable?"

Member grumbled and swore quietly and walked back to his bedroom. He got back into bed.

"Why don't you roll me a cigarette?" he said.

Jake took the package of makings from beside the bed and rolled him one. Member took it and lit it.

"You roll fucking awful cigarettes," he said.

"Look," Jake said, "let's go for a drive out in the country."

Member turned over and looked at him.

"Are you kidding?" he said.

He put his head down and took a drag of the cigarette.

20

"Let me have your car then."

"Jesus, just take the thing and let me sleep. The keys are in my pants."

"I found something in a magazine to show you," Jake said.

"Great, man, but later."

Jake took the keys and left. There wasn't any point in trying to talk to Member. Just drive north and look at the lakes and rocks and empty farms.

3

Where there was light (and in all things there was such light), she saw the hand of God marking out for her a way to go, even downward, until the final act of reconciliation that would take place at her breast which would there become a fountain of light, but only after such pain as she could never hope to tell. For months she had been clenched against the silence that was all He would give her until, clenched, held hard against this substance pain, stone world, world that seemed unspoken, she had battered the stone into light.

She drank from her teacup. Perhaps they would not come again now, were finished with their stupidities that did not touch her, only made her speech halt, stammer more, as if the impossibility of answering any question struck her tongue stiffer. She could not give them what they wanted, what she only knew as what must be rejected, the tawdry supposed facts when there is only one Fact. Perhaps it would be explained, but not by her. They must know that.

They would have her draw out some simple pattern that they could understand, but she could see in it only what was part of her battered world, was meant to lead her to the battering, like the quiet of wrong silences before she had met John and found silences they could share, the sung perfections at St. Mary Magdalen's where he would leave her to the accomplishment of peace. Now she must leave him to his own world, not understanding, not translating what he had lived away from mystery.

She went to the window and saw, outside it, the pear tree that survived by some unlikelihood in London, this close city, the tree where one day she had seen a single drop of rain on the side of a pear and light in that drop and where at other times she had seen the pale sunlight wash over all the pears that hung heavy among the leaves, the simplest blessedness, the pears growing in the walled yard, without care, falling useless to the ground, as the tree, like her flesh, without thought governed itself for living.

When the telephone rang, she knew what it would be, another newspaper or magazine wanting information that would feed and tease the pained closed appetites, and she answered, mute with stammering, and said only that she would not speak, not saying that she would not betray John by any speech of hers.

They walked out of the church together into streets that were already dark, for it was November, desperate grey cold that offered only the hope of snow. They walked down the street and turned the corner that led them back toward the university. As they walked, John took her hand.

"Margaret," he said, "I'll never be able to repay what you've done for me."

She would not let him speak about repayment.

"You're so wise," he said.

They walked on. As they walked, Margaret thought how

*what understanding she had was given to her, by her father,
by John's gift of care, by God's love.*

When the High Commissioner had called on her, he
had been worried about the indignity of the outcry,
troubled that he could not give her entire protection
from this, and Margaret could not explain that she
could do whatever was needed without pain from
what could be seen or said. This, if nothing else, she
had learned from her father. The lines drawn and
chosen gave what strength could ever be needed.

She had little sense of what all this could mean to
John or to the High Commissioner, what complex
loyalties were at issue or what betrayed, except the
simplest of loyalties to what is close and has been
accepted on trust.

What had John lived with? she wondered now, when
she was clenched against the stone, bearing only pain
at that time, given nothing but enough faith not to
give up demanding that there should be an answer
or at least that the question should be allowed to be
said fully. The power to ask was the one strength she
had then, but as she lived her battle, John was left
somewhere behind except for the merest habits of
speech and careful action. Then came what they called
his betrayal, his act of calling out that there must be
a question to be asked and foolishly, as worldly as
worldly, he thought that a choice of man from man
could answer what was beyond choice and beyond
man, that any calling to account could be more than a
show, a mockery of what could be said or understood
in silence and in the hands of God.

4

On his way back into Kingston, Jake drove past the big prison. It always amazed him to look at the high walls and towers, to see the guards walking along the walls with their rifles.

People talked about political prisoners in Cuba, but it had always seemed to Jake that all prisoners were political prisoners. In Cuba they imprisoned the rich, in Canada the poor. The details of how it was done hardly mattered.

Jake glanced at the grey walls as they disappeared in the rear-view mirror and drove on. When he got back to his room, there was a message pinned on his door. It was in Willy's handwriting.

I heard your phone ringing so I went in and answered it. It was your mother and she wants you to phone her. She sounds nice.

W

Jake took down the note and carried it into the bright, cluttered room with him. It must have something to do with John.

He picked up the phone and dialed the operator. He knew that if he took the trouble to look up the area code he could dial directly to her number, but he didn't feel like looking it up. In a couple of minutes he had his mother on the phone.

"Hello Mamma," he said. "It's Jacob."

"Who was that girl that answered the telephone?"

"She lives upstairs. She heard it ringing and came in."

There was a pause while his mother took this in.

"You should lock your door."

"I don't have anything worth stealing."

"This morning a policeman came to the house," his mother said.

"Did he tell you about John? That he's disappeared?"

"What do they mean disappeared?"

"I don't know, Mamma. I guess he just hasn't showed up at home or at work. They say he's a spy, but they wouldn't tell me how they know that."

"I want you to go to England and find him."

"I've got no money," Jake said. "And how could I find him?"

"I have enough money. They tell me my son is gone somewhere, and they can do nothing. You go and see Margaret and find out."

"Look, Mamma," Jake said, "you better let me think about it. I'll call you back this afternoon. OK?"

"All right. You get ready to go and phone me."

Jake hung up. He hadn't imagined before how upset his mother would be, and how little the mountie who told her could explain. She hadn't read a newspaper for as long as Jake could remember, and although she had a television set that John had bought her, she seldom watched it and never watched the news. For her, the events of the day were those she heard about from her old friends around the town, gossip about families, children, businesses of those she knew. Once Jake had asked her to tell him about his father's life in Russia, but she threw up her hands and disclaimed all knowledge of her husband's affairs.

The idea of going to England was an appealing one. Jake was bored with his classes, and it would be pleasant to take off and see a new country. He couldn't get over the idea that it would be a waste of his mother's money. What could he tell her that the police couldn't?

But there might be things that they wouldn't tell her or that Margaret wouldn't tell them. Certainly there might be something he could explain to his mother better than some big bastard of a mountie could. He was still skeptical about going as a favour to his mother, just because he did want to go, wanted to go badly when he thought about it.

Jake felt the pain in his stomach coming back. He made himself a sandwich and coffee and sat down with a book, a text for a politics course that he and Member liked to call Status Quo 368. There was a class in a couple of hours, and Jake decided that if he got the next couple of chapters read, he'd go for a change.

He did attend the class and regretted it. Someone spent an hour reading an endless boring paper on the Mackenzie King-Lord Byng affair, and by the end of it, Jake was ready to scream. At one point he promised himself that if there was one more set of quotations cancelling each other out, he'd let himself get up and leave. There was, and he didn't, but he was feeling pretty grouchy by the end of the class. He went to the Union with a few others and had coffee and a piece of pie, but he didn't say two words all the time they were there. One of the girls had always intrigued him and seemed to be trying to draw him into the conversation, but he looked at the clothes she wore, a skirt made of squares of green and brown suede, a green blouse tucked in tightly at the waist to exaggerate the pointed shape that her brassière gave her breasts, and he decided he wasn't really interested. He couldn't live in that landscape. So he just mumbled and grunted and ignored her.

While he was finishing his coffee, Jake remembered that he hadn't phoned back to his mother. He hadn't really made up his mind either. The old woman had never told him how much money she had, but she still went out cleaning a couple of days a week, and

Jake assumed that she didn't have much and tried not to ask her for anything. A few times when he was desperate he'd got a few dollars, but to take several hundred for the trip to England seemed too much. The simplest thing was to leave it up to her. If she wanted to spend her money sending him to England, he was glad to go.

He got up from the table, waved a sort of goodbye and left the Union. As soon as he got home, he phoned his mother and asked her if she was sure she wanted him to go. She wanted him to leave as soon as possible and had been checking with a friend who was a travel agent, so she already knew the cost of the fare and had a money order ready to send. When Jake explained to her that it would take time to get a passport, she surprised him again by saying that the passport people must know about John, and if he phoned and explained, they would get his passport ready in a hurry.

"OK, Mamma," Jake said. "I'll phone this afternoon and see what I can do."

When he hung up, he tried to decide where in Ottawa he should phone. There was nothing about John in the papers yet, so there was no use in assuming that everyone in External would know. The more he thought about it, the more he thought he might as well start at the top. He picked up the phone and dialed the long distance operator.

"I want to call Ottawa," he told her. "The Deputy Minister's Office in the Department of External Affairs."

The operator began a series of dialings and inquiries. Jake tried to roll a cigarette while he was waiting, but he found it hard to do while keeping the receiver at his ear, and he spilled a lot of tobacco on the floor.

The call finally got through to a secretary who seemed a bit hostile until Jake told her his name. Then she got interested and told him to hold on while she went to check. In about half a minute, Jake heard a voice identify itself as the Deputy Minister. Jake explained that he and his mother had just heard the strange message about John, and that he needed a passport if he was to go to England for his mother.

"Well, Mr. Martens," the voice said, "I don't know that you could really do much good by going to England. We'll certainly keep you and your mother informed."

Jake had the impression of a voice coming from a million miles away, not a bad connection, just something in the voice.

"It's very important to her," Jake said. "She's an old woman and I think it would make her feel a lot better if I went."

"I see. Well I don't know if we can do anything over the weekend, but if you could bring all your documents to Ottawa on Monday, we could probably get it ready in an hour or so."

"Great," Jake said. "I'll be there Monday."

When he hung up the phone, Jake felt a little breathless. He wasn't used to observing real power in action. He understood, all of a sudden, why some people would do anything to get into that kind of position. You snapped your fingers, and it was done. He wondered if Lord Acton had watched that kind of executive power, if he knew the pull in the guts of knowing that your orders would be obeyed, or whether he'd just sat home with his history books charting the downward progress of kings and princes and writing QED. at the end of each.

What about Lord Acton's servants? He must have had them, every British gentleman did. When he told his man to black his boots or had his maid fetch tea, did he say to himself, "Careful, Acton, power, you know, all power tends. . . . Don't bring that tea, girl. I'll make it myself. Lest I become corrupt." And the

28

girl would stare at him and think that the old boy was crazy this time for sure.

If I wish it done, it will be done.

And what was their argument? That without that kind of power nothing would get done at all. But was that such a bad thing?

Jake got up from the chair, still considering the ominous sense of power that he'd got on the phone, and went out to the Post Office for a passport application. He stopped on the way to arrange about having a photograph taken and got to the Post Office just before it closed.

When he got back to his room, he started to fill in the form, then put it away, picked up the page of the magazine with the sentence he wanted to show Member, stuck it in his back pocket and went out. He drove the car over to Member's place, parked it and walked up the stairs. Two or three people were in the room talking about the demonstration.

"Listen," Member said when he walked in, "are you going with the group at the city hall or the other one."

"I think I'll go to the sit-in at Buckingham Palace," Jake said.

Member looked at him.

"Are you stoned?" he said.

"No. I'm going to England next week."

"C'mon Jake, cut out the bullshit."

"Really. I'd tell you the whole story but you wouldn't believe it."

"Tell me anyway."

"You know my brother, he's in External."

"Yeah."

"Well he's disappeared in London. They say he's a spy."

"You're right, I don't believe it," Member said. "You're not just stoned, you're so spaced you must have been shooting rat poison."

Jake started to laugh. He couldn't help it.

"It's true. This great big mountie came to tell me this morning."

Member just shook his head.

"Ask Willy. She was there."

"I wouldn't ask Willy what time it was and expect her to tell me the truth."

"OK," Jake said. "I admit it sounds wild, but really, this big son of a bitch of a mountie knocked on the door and said he'd come to tell me my brother had disappeared, and they thought he was a spy."

"You and Willy and the mountie," Member said, "and who was on top?"

"Go to hell," Jake said. "Do you want your fucking car keys?"

"Did you take Willy and the mountie for a drive?"

"No, I didn't," Jake said. He threw down the car keys. Member was still shaking his head.

"Are you really going to England?" someone said. Jake turned around. It was Al Sturgess, an American deserter who'd turned up in town at the beginning of the term.

"Yeah," Jake said. "I am."

"There's a buddy of mine in London, Don Hattersley. You should get in touch with him. You could probably crash there if you're stuck. I'll look up his address for you."

"You really won't be here for the demonstration?" Member said.

"Not a chance. My old lady's really uptight about the whole thing, and she wants me to go over and find him or something. I don't know what I'm supposed to find."

"The CIA," Al said. "They're everywhere."

Member ignored Jake now. They'd been arguing for days about whether anyone who was charged at the demonstration should accept bail, and the group

30

in the room went on arguing for the next half hour while Jake listened without speaking. It seemed he was no longer part of it. Finally they decided to get the whole group together to discuss it again.

Jake could see the excitement starting to get hold of Member until he found it hard to sit still and kept scratching his cheek and standing up only to sit back down again. When the others left, Member turned to Jake.

"It's going to work, isn't it? It's going to work."

"But what's it going to prove?"

"Jesus Christ we talked about that last night. That it's all one big fuck-up, the city, the university, the whole works."

"But you don't have an issue."

"Everything is an issue. The existence of the cops is an issue. Why shouldn't people get together and police their own streets, their own district?"

"Shit, you've got to attack where it will matter. You'll just be putting on a performance for the media freaks. It's the perfect way to get emasculated."

"Jake, you know what a pragmatist is? He's a guy who's so busy winning battles that he loses the war."

Jake took the clipping out of his jeans pocket.

"Look," he said. "I brought this specially for you."

He handed it over, Member looked at it and threw it down on the bed.

"Christ, I read that," he said. "The guy who wrote it is a university professor, for Christ's sake, another fucking liberal, whatever he likes to call himself. There's no difference now between changing society and defying it. The whole thing is so rigid that you've got to shake it up, make some cracks, make it possible for any real kind of change to take place. Defiance is the only real revolutionary act because defiance denies the fuckers all their assumptions. What do you want? To change a traffic light from that corner to this corner?

31

To get the old age pensioners a dollar a month while the cost of living goes up by two? That's not what people need, a little more money to be bored with, they need to get out from under all the fucking bullshit that we're all buried in, and that's why we've got to defy them. Like that fantastic slogan they had in France. *It is forbidden to forbid.* God, in Paris they must have had some idea of what it was like to be free, to have the feeling that you could turn to the guy next to you and say 'Let's change the world brother, let's you and me change the world,' and hear him say, 'OK brother, we'll do that.' And then go out to do it."

Member was nearly jumping up and down with excitement as he said this. He kept running his fat fingers through his hair. Jake always found him irresistible when he was like this.

"Defy society," Member said, "that's the one goddam thing we have to do, man. Defy all the bullshit."

"You make it sound good," Jake said.

"Christ," Member said. "By some kind of historical process, we're cut off from all the bullshit, it doesn't make sense to us anymore, and we've got to keep on shouting that it doesn't make sense until everyone says no it doesn't and decides that they're not going to take any more crap, that they're going to do what they want, and then it will all be so beautiful."

They were silent for a minute.

"Hey," Jake said, "I found an old log farm out there this afternoon. Fantastic, you know, this old log house and the old barns sitting there empty in the middle of miles of farmland."

"Jake," Member said, "there are times when I think you've got the soul of a bourgeois. All you really want to do is buy a little farm in the country and settle down to raised carrots and potatoes."

"Shit no, I don't want to own it. I don't want to keep anybody else off it. I want to live with the land.

32

To do some hard work that's worthwhile."

"What does history matter? We'll live with fucking nature and commune with God. Christ, Jake, nature's dead and God's dead; we all live in history now, and there's no way out. There's no easy way back." He stopped for a minute. "It's a nice old dream though, you're right about that. Shit, let's get stoned. I've got some of that good hash left."

"No," Jake said. "I don't much want to."

"When are you going to England?"

"A couple of days. I have to go up to Ottawa to get my passport fixed up in a hurry. You know I just phoned the Deputy Minister and told him who I was, and he promised to fix it up just like that."

"They must be really uptight about your brother."

"I guess so."

"It'll be great for you to see England. You should get that guy's address from Al."

"I will."

There was another silence.

"I think I'll take off," Jake said.

"OK, man, we'll see you before you go."

Jake nodded. There was something he wanted to say, but it wouldn't come. He left the room and walked down the dark staircase. He walked home the long way, thinking about what Member had said, and for the first time thinking about his brother really seriously, wondering where he was and how he felt about everything, why he'd disappeared, where he'd gone. It was all bewildering.

When he walked into his room, the light was on, and Willy was lying on the bed.

"What are you doing here?" he said.

"Well, that's hard to say. It's . . . well . . . it's . . . oh is it ever."

"You're pretty stoned," he said.

"I am so high . . . oh . . . am I so high. I don't think

33

I ever want to come down."

"What did you take?"

"There was some lightning . . . and some mescaline . . . and I think that's all."

"What are you doing here?"

"I thought I'd live here."

"You'll be living alone," Jake said. "I'm going to England."

"Jake," she said, "you're a shit."

5

Again this morning, as so often, she stood at the window to look out at the pear tree and beyond it to the house next door with its careful small yard where the roses still bloomed. She remembered her first visit to England, years before, leaving Canada, where nothing would grow until spring, and finding the roses here, greyed by wind and cloud, but continuing, and for her always calling to mind Christ and the hymn of Praetorius, Advent and Nativity, and then recalling her own child. Even now she couldn't remember him for more than a moment without a tightening all through her body as if the pain would return. She walked away from the window and looked for some small activity. She would wash the dishes she had used for breakfast, with some small salvation in this, in such a small action, and all actions, she thought now, even betrayal, even murder, were small and only momentary events, done and vanished.

When she had finished the task, she looked around

her, once again threatened by the memory of the child. At the window again, she looked down at the roses, especially one rose that was a clear dark red among the others of all rose colours. Her eyes drifted down again and again to that single flower, now almost dead, the petals beginning to curl awry. The dark rose, the colour of blood, moved a little in the wind, like blood blown into the air to die in the light. She wondered now if John were somewhere dead, his blood married to the air or his body tumbled to ruin, the body that she could never perfectly hold, her love stuttering like her tongue.

She went to the bookcase and took down the Bible. Even as she held it in her hands there was a kind of comfort in knowing that it would draw her away from her pain. When she opened it, content to read whatever words came in front of her eyes, she found a loose scrap of paper inside, with writing on it that she recognized as John's. At the top of the paper was an address, and below a series of short notes that she did not read. The familiar writing brought her suddenly close to him, as if he had walked into the house, but she closed the book with the piece of paper still inside it and sat in a chair with the book held in her lap. She wouldn't read what John had written there unless he returned and showed it to her, for she had promised him in his absence that she wouldn't question his actions, and thinking this, she remembered the prying curiosity of the police, all the papers they had taken from the filing cabinet. They hadn't looked in the Bible, and she wondered now if this poor last scrap of paper was something they would call important, if they would say she ought to give it to them, let them read what she would not.

Her father had come in later than usual, and his face, always serious, looked almost haggard. Margaret had finished her

35

homework and was reading a book, but she got up and helped her mother make his supper, and she brought it to him. He took it without thanking her, and she was surprised and hurt, for she thought he must be angry, but he didn't speak, and Margaret went back to her book. She couldn't concentrate. She heard her mother go into the dining-room with two cups of tea, settle herself at the table and begin to talk to him, making small talk about the events of the day, particularly a telephone conversation with a friend of theirs who had been in hospital. Her father didn't answer. Margaret found her whole concentration was on the voices in the dining-room, as if something terrible were about to happen there. She heard her mother ask if something was wrong. Her father said yes, and no more. There was a silence. Margaret knew what her mother was feeling, wanting to know what the trouble was, wanting to ask, but knowing that she could not, that he would speak when he wanted to. The silence went on and on. At last her father spoke.

"Ask Margaret to play the piano," he said.

Her mother came in.

"Your father wants you to play the piano for him."

Margaret went to the piano and began to play a Bach Prelude. In a few minutes her father came into the room and sat down with his tea. When Margaret glanced over at him, she saw he had put his head back and closed his eyes. His teacup was resting on his knee, and a bit of steam rose into the air.

She played for him for half an hour, and he sat without speaking. Finally, he stood up, thanked her, and went out into the kitchen where her mother was baking. He spoke to her and went out. Margaret wanted to ask her mother what was wrong, but she always hesitated to get into serious conversation with her mother. They didn't communicate easily, and both preferred to keep to small matters of daily concern.

Margaret went back to her book and read with little attention until it was time for bed. As she lay in bed, she *found herself wondering what had caused her father's distress, imagining vaguely terrible disasters and disgraces.*

In the morning, her father seemed more himself, still a bit preoccupied, but able to chat normally with them. Margaret was made even more curious by this, wondering whether the thing worrying him was over or whether he'd simply accustomed himself to it.

When she got to school that morning, there were a number of strange rumours about someone's father being arrested, and by the end of the day, the newspapers and every conversation were full of the stories of the arrests. The name of Gouzenko was everywhere. Margaret bought a paper for herself on the way home from school and found among those arrested the names of a couple of acquaintances of her father and one old school friend, a man he had once been close to, although recently they hadn't had a great deal of contact. Her father must have known the night before that the arrests were going to take place.

Remembering that day, Margaret wondered if there was ever a moment when he might have warned his friend, might have felt some small temptation to phone on the strength of their shared past and tell him he must run if he was to avoid arrest. It seemed to her impossible that he should feel such a temptation, but she knew that just as she had missed something in John, so in her father, there might have been, somewhere beyond the rectitude a momentary wonder, a shiver of possibility. They had grown up together in the same town, teacher's son and minister's son, two of the few who were to be sent away at whatever cost, to be educated at a university and to make their way from there, poor enough, but assured by their own family history, by the years of accumulated expectation that they would do well, picking up some small skills to carry them along from year to year until they reached some settled place, as a teacher, doctor, lawyer or, as

37

her father had, a civil servant, poor for years, but differently now, with a respected steady poverty that gradually disappeared, leaving only the habit of careful accounting. The other boy, the minister's son, had pursued what seemed a similar path, but had added up the accounts differently so that her father had been faced with the accusation of treason against his old friend. She had wanted to ask her father about that, and about his friend, what had led him, what his reasons were, but it was one of those subjects that she couldn't mention to him. She wondered now what her father would have said of John's actions, whatever it all came to that he had done, and more and more, it seemed to her, in a poor blind way.

She opened the Bible again and looked at the single piece of paper, moved once more by the familiarity of the handwriting, the sense of John's closeness. Margaret took the piece of paper in her hands and folded it in half, closed the book and set it down, then walked to the kitchen, set the paper alight and dropped it in the sink, then stood by the sink and looked down at the small flame that spread its ruin across the white page, her strongest feeling a regret at the further separation from John in the loss of this scrap.

She was not much troubled by what judgment men could make of this, although it almost seemed as if her father were watching her act. For him, as for John, acts were only acts and disastrously they mattered. John had held a faith that the world's way could be changed, that a step in the dark could be known as a step toward light. Perhaps he would return to explain all this, but if he did, he would be punished, for no court would care that she had some small sense of what he meant to say by what he did, that she could under-stand his need, for they could only take the words of the law and make them into actions simply and literally, for the law did not know the heart and soul, but like

John, lived in the world of what was done, while for her it was hard to say even that a thing was done; to raise her arm or to walk to the window was an action, but to beseech God silently as she sat in her chair was not.

When the telephone rang, she expected another reporter with some meaningless question, and she held herself stiff against the absurdity of what she must go through. The voice was Canadian and young, identifying itself with a name both strange and familiar so that she stupidly didn't know until he told her that it was John's brother Jacob. He was in London to learn more about John and what he had done. She asked him if he would stay with her in the extra room of the flat, and although he was slow to accept, he couldn't have much money and seemed relieved finally that he could accept and have a place to go.

They reached the town late in the afternoon, after a couple of hours' bus ride from Toronto. It was a strange kind of day, somewhere between winter and spring, with a dust of new snow on top of streets that held only traces of the winter snow. It had begun to melt, but now frozen again. A friend of John's family had met them at the bus and driven them to the house. The sun had not gone down, but its light seemed to exaggerate the bareness of the trees. They drove for a few blocks and pulled up in a driveway beside a small frame house. John took the cases out of the trunk of the car, and the man who drove them shook hands in silence and went away.

They went in the back door of the house, into the kitchen. John's mother was standing at the stove stirring something when they came in, and as she turned toward them, Margaret felt suddenly that she liked this woman for some reason that she couldn't state. The woman smiled and came toward them, kissed John on the cheek and nodded shyly as John introduced Margaret to her. She had a round face and her hair was pulled into a bun at the back of her head. She organized their sleeping arrangements, asking with each suggestion if it was all right, and addressing herself to Margaret, as if her opinion was the one that mattered most.

When they were about to go upstairs, a small boy appeared in the kitchen door. He was thin and sad. John greeted him in a friendly way, but it seemed that they didn't know each other well and had little to say to each other.

The mother gave Jacob a cookie and told him they would be having supper soon, and he disappeared into a dark corner of the living-room to play with a wooden truck. He hardly seemed to come out of the corner for the next two days. Someone came and took him away for the time of the funeral, but even when he was in the house, he kept very much to himself. Margaret tried to talk to him once or twice, but couldn't draw him out. He answered questions by saying as little as possible, although he did not seem resentful, just to have nothing to say to her.

That night John went to the funeral home with two of his uncles, men that he had never mentioned to Margaret and seemed hardly to know, and Margaret was left with his mother. At first, the old woman tried to treat Margaret as a guest who needed special attention, but when she began to wash the supper dishes, Margaret insisted on helping, and the old woman let her, relaxing and beginning to treat her like a younger member of the family. She didn't seem to be greatly saddened by her husband's death, at least on the surface, and she had tried to refuse the help of one of John's aunts who wanted to stay with her for the evening. Margaret supposed she found it easier to keep working, not to let the death change the pattern of her life, and she noticed during the evening that whenever the aunt tried, in her awkward way, to express sympathy, the bereaved woman simply directed the conversation another way.

As the three of them sat and talked, Margaret learned a great deal about John's family background, the adventures and sorrows of obscure relatives she would never hear mentioned again. Sometimes she wondered if the two women didn't resent her presence as that of an outsider, but John's mother

40

*seemed to dislike the aunt a little, and that made her turn
the conversation toward Margaret whenever she could. Still,
Margaret was relieved when John got back.*

It was still odd for her to think of John's brother here
in London and coming to her soon to ask questions
that she couldn't answer for him any more than for the
High Commissioner or the newspapers. He would want
to know what it all meant, to face his brother or his
brother's ghost and say Brother, what news? What
wisdom?

She went to the closet to get sheets for the extra bed,
took out the crisp white sheets that she loved to handle,
that seemed an emblem of something pure and simple,
spread them on the bed with the feeling that she was
falling into their whiteness as into some eternal snow.
She enjoyed the skill with which she folded the corners
so that the sheets lay flat and smooth over the bed.
Margaret lit the gas fire to dry the room and warm it,
the fire too catching her attention, like another emblem
side by side with the sheets, the blue translucence of
the fire and the white sheets, there were wonders in
these, and she found herself speculating about the
boy who would come here, what he would see in these
things.

She had little food on hand, and as she dressed to
go out, she felt both ordinary and strange to be going
out into the world that knew something or believed
it did about John and his actions. She could still,
perhaps, go on her way, unknown, one woman among
millions walking along the streets to the nearest shops,
buying, walking back, who, if she were known to
those around might be greeted with sympathy or anger.

She walked down always with the sense that it might
never stop, that she might descend into an underworld
where years of nightmares waited for her, where the
child would die again and again in her arms. She walked

41

into the street quickly, as if the magic of movement could cleanse her and take her away from that dream, of all things, the one that she could least bear. It seemed to strike at her head like blows, pressing her down till, clenched like a fist, she faced the stone world and beat on it, saying over to herself even now as she walked the street. Out of the depths have I cried to thee, O Lord, until the repetition of the prayer softened her, eased the force of the blows at her head.

She slowed her pace a little and looked around her, astonished, as always at such moments, that there should still be people in the world, that men and women walked on around her. The young girls hurt her with the sight of their youth and the clothes they wore, the skirts so short, the gaiety of them spurious, not joyful, harried by the need to draw men's eyes, to do whatever they thought would make them real, for they believed in nothing, least of all themselves. They were so young and favoured with beauty that she knew she might only be jealous, even now when she thought herself beyond any such thing.

What she liked most, as she walked along the street, was to see people talk happily to one another, to see them smile, almost to believe that there was love given in this, that those who smiled would not betray their friends for some small gain, and she watched for happiness as some men watched for money.

As she walked, it seemed to her that a man was walking behind her, following her, and she grew angry, for she couldn't endure that suspicion should be turned on her, walked aware of him, and finally in her anger, turned when he came close and shouted that if he didn't go away, she would find a constable.

The man turned away as if he had business and did not know who she might be, but likely, she knew, turned aside for only a moment, pretending to go away then again following her, for whatever wrong and stupid reasons, as if all things now were suspect, that no-one could be simple.

6

For the first few minutes as he rode on the bus from the airport, Jake found that he was trying to see everything at once, as if he could digest England in ten minutes by noticing every detail of this ride, but he soon realized the foolishness of this and relaxed, just letting the city move past him without attempting to see anything very clearly.

Member and Willy had driven him to Montreal to catch the plane, and Jake remembered his last sight of them at the airport, Member in clothes that looked like something from a charity and Willy in a wide-brimmed Spanish hat, a black velvet dress with a gold belt and high black boots. They made a funny pair.

Jake had phoned Margaret before getting on the bus, and he was glad he'd been able to arrange to stay with her for a few days because he didn't have much money. He supposed he could make all the inquiries that were any use to his mother in a fairly short time, but he hoped to have a chance to see some of London and get in touch with Al Sturgess's friend. He had the address in his wallet, and he'd got the impression from Al that his friend Hattersley was already pretty active here. In fact, from the way Al told it, it seemed that Hattersley had got off the plane and started demonstrating before he reached the bottom of the stairs.

Jake looked at his watch. It was still set on Canadian time and said ten after five. He turned it ahead and thought again of those he'd left the day before. His rent was paid for a month in advance, so he'd given Willy the key of his place and told her she could stay there until he came back.

When they reached the air terminal, Jake waited impatiently for his bag which had come on a trailer behind the bus. It was an old rucksack, and when it came round on the circling table, he took it by the straps and carried it out to the line of cabs.

It felt strange to Jake to be getting into one of the big English cabs and giving the driver the address, even to be here in London at all. He wasn't used to riding in taxis, in fact he wasn't sure whether he'd ever been in one before he left home to go to university. He and his mother didn't have the money to travel far, and they lived in a small town where there was no place they couldn't walk. Even at university, the only times Jake had been able to afford a taxi were when he shared it with a group who were all going somewhere together. All this went through his mind as he sat on the leather seat and watched the streets go past.

Jake saw the name of the square where Margaret lived as they turned a corner, and he was a little shocked to realize that they had arrived already. The cab stopped at a large house near the end of the square.

When Jake reached the door, he pressed the bell for the upper flat and stood waiting with his rucksack at his feet. In a few moments he heard footsteps inside, and the door opened.

"Come in," Margaret said, smiling almost shyly. "Ah . . . ah . . . " her mouth struggled with the sound. "Ah . . . I just got back from shopping."

She led him up the carpeted stairway. Jake was about to tell her how strange it felt to be here, but much of the strangeness was because of John, and it seemed best to wait until she spoke of him.

The door on the landing was open when they reached it, and Margaret walked in and let the way to a large living-room. There was a stuffed sofa, and near it was a stuffed chair. Both were upholstered in a striking material with large birds and trees on a pale cream background. Above the sofa were several military prints. The other furniture in the room was wooden, chairs and small tables that Jake could identify as expensive even though he knew nothing about furniture.

"Is this all yours?" he said, "Or did you leave your furniture in Canada?"

"We le . . . left most of our furniture in storage. Just a few of the smaller thi . . . thi . . . things are our own. I'll just put on the g . . . g . . . gas fire and show you your room."

She took a package of matches from a metal box on the mantel and lit the gas. Jake found that he was labouring through each sentence she spoke with her, wanting to help by saying words for her, almost falling off the chair in his eagerness to get the sentence done so they could both relax. He wondered if she stammered as much when she talked to John, and whether John had ever got used to it so that he didn't constantly feel that he wanted to finish words for her.

She led him down the hall to a small bedroom where there was another gas fire burning. The walls were pale brown and there were several old prints of birds and flowers.

"Ah . . . ah . . . ah . . . I made a bed for you here. Do you want to ha . . . ha . . . have a sleep now?"

"No," Jake said. "I didn't get much sleep on the plane, but I don't really feel like sleeping now. I'll just unpack some of my things and get washed up."

She showed him the bathroom and told him to take a bath if he wanted.

45

"I might do that," Jake said. "It's probably the best thing after sleeping in your clothes."

"Ah . . . ah . . . I'll put the kettle on for tea."

Jake started to unpack the rucksack. There wasn't a lot in it, mostly some warmer clothes that everybody warned him to bring. He took out a couple of books.

He soon had everything unpacked, and he rolled up the rucksack and put it under the bed. It was a pleasant feeling to be carrying everything he needed in one bag. He liked the feeling of self-sufficiency this gave him. When he thought about everything he'd left in his room in Canada, it amused him to think of the amount of rubbish that was there, that he seemed to collect somehow. Life was a process of accumulation; you chose one thing, another, clothes to wear, books to read, old postcards that you saved for an address, a shirt you once liked, saved things until there was a danger that all these things you'd chosen controlled you, and suddenly you had to go away or burn them all to escape and start over with only your bare self and the immediate necessities of life.

Jake found his little red notebook in his jacket pocket and wrote in it the bit of poetry he'd made up on the plane.

> I have a friend, Earth
> and I have another, Sky.
> Who is my father?

Sometimes Jake wondered why he recorded all his scraps of poetry. He didn't take them seriously, but the little book was almost full of his scribbles.

Jake put down the book and turned to look out the window, aware of feeling tired and dirty. It was a full day since he'd put on these clothes. He decided to get a bath and walked into the next room where Margaret had indicated the tub was.

Jake turned on the tap, and the hot water steamed

into the tub. He wondered how much of his feeling of strangeness was due to the disorientation of the long flight, the sleeplessness and time change. At home it was not yet time to be awake. Willy would still be asleep in his bed. Jake wondered whether she would be alone there. She might have taken Member back with her, although she'd never liked him much. Still, she was unpredictable. It was just as well that Jake wasn't too attached to the things he'd left in his room, because with Willy staying there a lot of them might be lost or ruined by the time he got back.

He took off his clothes and got into the long tub. Jake was so thin that he couldn't sit comfortably in a bathtub. There was no protection for the base of his spine. He lay down in the warm water, sleepy and relaxed now, and stayed there until he began to doze off, then roused himself, washed and got out into the chilly air of the room.

When he'd finished dressing, he pushed back his hair and walked down the hall looking for Margaret. She was in the kitchen.

"Just sit down in the luh . . . lounge," she said, "and ah . . . ah . . . I'll bring some tea in for both of us."

Jake went into the room across the hall and sat down in one of the big soft chairs. On the wall near him, beside a bookshelf, was a crucifix, just a small plain black one, but it shocked him by its presence there and his eyes kept coming back to it.

It didn't surprise him, when he considered it, that Margaret might be religious, but he wondered if John had been. He was suddenly aware that he was thinking of John as someone who was dead.

Jake's eyes were drawn to the crucifix again, and he tried to remember John clearly. What he saw was a round and self-satisfied little man with a rather pompous small voice and glasses with dark rims that seemed somehow his chief point of contact with the world. A

47

kind complacent man who had given Jake money, not only for his fees, but once or twice spontaneously sending a money order in the mail. He must know from his own experience that Jake wouldn't have enough money and wouldn't want to take it from their mother.

Still, it must surely be Margaret who had hung the crucifix there.

Margaret came into the room with the tea and some biscuits. She gave Jake a cup and put a plate of biscuits on the table beside him.

Outside the window, Jake could see the branches of a pear tree and beyond them, one corner of a church against a grey sky. He didn't know quite how to ask her about John and wondered for a moment if he should say nothing and just make do with what he could learn from the External Affairs people.

Margaret looked up from her tea, and for a moment their eyes met, but she looked away and out the window. Jake had noticed in that moment that her eyes were a strange pale brown. She looked back toward him, not at him.

"Ah . . . ah . . . ah . . ." she struggled to form the words, "ah . . . I suppose you've come to find out more about John."

"For my mother," Jake said. "She phoned me after the mounties had been to see her. She didn't know what to make of it all, so she wanted me to come and see what I could find out."

She took a drink of her tea, and for a moment, Jake thought that was all she was going to say. But she looked up again.

"I'll tell you what I can," she said. It was strange to hear the sentence spoken without any halt.

She told Jake that the previous Wednesday night, John had not come home when she expected him, but that at first she hadn't been upset because he often stayed late at the office, and even when she began to worry, she had waited and hadn't phoned anyone until morning when she had phoned his office and was told that he had left the previous night at his usual time. No-one had seen him return to the office during the evening. She told them he had not been home, and they phoned the police. Later that day someone phoned Canada House from a hostel south of the river and said that a Mr. Martens had left a briefcase full of papers, some that indicated that he was on the staff of the High Commissioner. The police had gone to the hostel and collected the papers and within a few hours they came to the flat and asked to look through John's possessions.

Margaret didn't describe her feelings about any of this, but as she told the story, stopped again and again by the painful stammer, Jake could sense the moments that had been hardest for her, and this was clearly one of them, when the police, without giving her any real explanation, had asked to go through John's things and had broken open a locked filing cabinet.

They had taken more papers and a camera, she said, and a couple of hours later, the High Commissioner had arrived to see her and to tell her that the papers included some kind of journal that indicated that John had been a spy.

"Did they show it to you?"

She shook her head.

"They said they cuh . . . cuh . . . couldn't show it to anyone." She sat quiet for a few seconds, pressing her hands on the arms of her chair.

Then she went on to tell him how the next day the newspapers had started to phone her asking for information about John, and again Jake could see it was painful for her even to tell this.

She stopped for a moment and finished her tea, then set the cup on the table beside her. Jake thought she was finished now, but in a moment she went on, telling

49

him what the High Commissioner had said about John being unbalanced and troubled, mentioning the death of their child. Jake had almost forgotten the child's death, something he had heard about indirectly through his mother, first the surprise of the birth when neither of them was young anymore and then the death shortly after, told to him second-hand so that he had pitied them, but only at such a distance that the whole thing had not been very real.

"Do you think someone at Canada House would talk to me about it?"

"Ah . . . ah . . . I'm sure they would. Why duh . . . duh . . . don't you call?" She seemed relieved to escape and indicated a phone in the corner of the room. She wrote the number on a piece of paper for him. Jake looked at her as she stood there with her back to him, her brown hair, the green sweater and tweed skirt emphasizing the heaviness of her body, and he felt as if he were looking at her from the surface of the moon or from some distant point in time.

He went to the phone, and she left the room so that he was alone to make his call.

He dialed the number.

"Office of the High Commissioner," the girl's voice said.

"My name is Jacob Martens. John Martens, my brother, was on the staff there."

"Just a minute," she said.

Jake stood holding the receiver until a man's voice came on the line.

"Allington here, who's speaking please?"

"My name's Jake Martens. John Martens is my brother."

There was a pause.

"Where are you calling from?"

"I'm in London. My mother wanted me to come over and try to get a bit more information about what

50

happened. She was very upset."

"Yes, of course. Where are you staying?"

"At Margaret's place. For now anyway."

"I see. Well look, Mr. Martens, I'm not sure how much help I can be to you. You understand there's a good deal of classified material involved here, but you come in tomorrow afternoon about two and we'll have a chat. Is that all right?"

"OK," Jake said. "Tomorrow afternoon."

He hung up the phone. Something about the conversation left him with a nasty feeling. He sat down in a chair and started to look at a magazine from the table beside him, but within a couple of minutes he found his eyes closing.

There was no point in falling asleep in the chair, so he went out and found Margaret in the kitchen where she was washing the cups and told her that he would have a short sleep after all. He mentioned the appointment for the next afternoon, but she only nodded. He wanted to tell her about his feeling after the phone call, but he decided not to. It was strange though, how he trusted her immediately, as if their relationship in the past had been much closer.

In the bedroom he took off his boots and lay down. He fell asleep quickly, and when he woke it was the middle of the afternoon, but he felt as if he had hardly closed his eyes. He couldn't remember dreaming at all. He was tempted to sleep longer, but he roused himself, washed in cold water to wake himself and decided to go out and look around the neighbourhood.

Margaret was in the big room sitting on the sofa with a book, and when he put his head in to tell her he was going out, she told him that she'd left a plate of sandwiches in the kitchen for him.

"That's great," he said, "but look, don't worry about feeding me. It's enough trouble for you just having me here. I'll get myself some food now and then."

51

"It's no trouble," she said. "Ih . . . ih . . . it's quite nice to have someone to look after. I need to k . . . k . . . keep busy. Here's a set of k . . . keys you can use. In case ah . . . ah . . . I have to go out."

Jake took the keys and went across to the kitchen. He found the sandwiches and stood looking out the window as he ate them. Then he went out.

As he walked down the street away from the house, there was a long narrow park beside him. Jake walked up to one of the locked gates in the fence that surrounded it and saw the notice that said its use was reserved for those who lived in the square. Between the trees, on a path half-covered by fallen leaves, he saw a child riding on some kind of little car while his young mother sat on a bench nearby and watched him.

Jake walked to the end of the square where the traffic was heavy and noisy. He went down the street and turned back up behind the square, walking by the side of a large church, trying to recognize the back of Margaret's apartment. There was a second church behind the first, and he walked through the churchyard where a few flowers bloomed in the dark air.

Jake had thought before of Margaret as a kind of spirit haunting John, and even when he'd been in her flat, there was a strangeness that he couldn't explain. Everything she said seemed to come from far away. Jake thought over their conversation as he walked on through the nearby streets.

He turned back toward Margaret's flat. He went down a mews that was strangely empty as he moved toward the pub at the foot. When he was about halfway along, he heard a noise, and looking up, saw eight or ten geese not far above the rooftops flying slowly toward the river, honking only now and then.

Something in the sequence of things he'd seen made Jake remember an afternoon years ago at home, when he'd run straight from school to a park where he liked

52

to play football with the high-school boys, had played for over an hour and then fallen badly and split his lip open. His shirt was covered with blood, and the lip hurt him as he walked home, no longer crying, but sniffling a little and feeling cold as the sun disappeared and it began to get dark. As he walked along the street toward home, wondering what his mother would say about his nose and bloody shirt, he heard a clamouring noise above him, and looking up, saw a huge flock of geese, probably the biggest flock he'd ever seen, high up in the air in a couple of interlocking V shapes, passing the town as they flew south along the river.

Jake walked along the mews to the end and wondered if his brother was alive somewhere in this city.

7

The burning future. What I am not. The weight of possibility.

I felt the need to start this journal to explain myself to myself, to keep track of my development, for whatever reason, to write things down, to keep a record.

It's now almost two years since my son died. He was hardly my son really, just a baby four months old, pleasantly warm and dependent. Margaret would arrange his time-table so that when I got home from the office he would be awake, and I'd hold him and be surprised each time at the strength of my feeling for him, a son who had been born so late.

We had deliberately not had children until after we

were thirty and felt that we were ready, had a house in a good neighbourhood in Ottawa, seemed settled.

Twice Margaret lost a baby at an early stage of pregnancy. The first time was in France, and we blamed the carefree French doctor for it and didn't worry much afterward. The second was in Ottawa. It happened in the middle of the day that time, and I drove from the office to the hospital and waited while they got the haemorrhage under control, sitting with the oddly assorted people who are always found waiting in hospitals.

We hesitated to try a third time to have a child, but Margaret wanted one so badly that her doctor said yes. This time the child was born alive, apparently healthy, and he seemed a kind of completion to the mundane, but rich and pleasant life that we led. I held him in my arms and smiled, and Margaret lived for him entirely. I told her once that she had been reborn when that child came, and it was true.

I didn't question much in those days. There seemed no point to it. Life had a kind of inevitability, and I would know in advance what would be expected of me and what I would do. It all seemed very simple. The mask I wear now is the face I wore then. The first thing I was told was not to change. My first act of commitment to the future was to will the continuation of my past. To seem to be what I had always been, straightforward and dedicated, modestly ambitious, a bland vulgar fool like all the rest.

One morning Margaret got up, and the child was dead in his crib. The doctors couldn't explain it, they only know that it happens with a certain statistical regularity. They have suspicions, but nothing more.

Margaret was destroyed. Nothing less dramatic would be true. She has not fully existed since that morning.

Apart from the effect on me of her reaction, I found myself, for weeks and months afterward, affected by the death. The blow was less immediate for me, less entire, but now my whole life began to look different. We would never have another child, that was clear. Margaret had always been restrained, almost frigid, and now she was entirely shut up in herself.

A single evening. We sat there, Daniel and I, drunk at three o'clock in the morning. I remember that I got up and walked to the window and looked out over the smooth lawn, black now, and past the black trees to the house opposite. I knew the people who lived there, not well, but I knew them, and as I stood there, I thought of the two of them silent in their bed. I had once caught a glimpse of their bedroom as I found my way to the toilet during a cocktail party, and I could remember a large double bed, a white bedspread and an oil painting of a pale landscape hanging over it, and I could imagine the two ageing bodies asleep there. I closed my eyes.

"Daniel," I said, without turning around, "how do you manage? How do you keep on? You're a poet and poets are supposed to be wise. Tell me what to think at three o'clock in the morning."

I turned and looked at him. He was staring into his drink, his head lowered so that I could see the fringe of hair at the back of the bald skull.

"Don't just shrug it off," I said, "Why do you write? There must be something important to you, something that matters."

He didn't look up.

"It's a habit," he said. "Like smoking. You start when you're young and you never get over it." He finished his drink.

I looked back out the window.

"Here we are," I said, "two men who have money, education, are believed to be intelligent, almost important. And at three in the morning we're a little drunk and neither one of us has a single splendid or witty thing to say. That's pathetic."

I haven't worked at this for a week. My time has been taken up with a great variety of foolish affairs at the office, most of them matters of no importance, with dozens of phone calls and memoes flying between us and Grosvenor Square to no purpose.

I am waiting for contact with the new man. His code name is Simon. Perhaps they are pleased with the things I've begun to get them.

Now two days later. I have heard nothing more, but I can wait quite patiently because I know this matters.

Can't account for the passage of time, for the endless way everything dragged on then, how each day began and ended like every other day. Every day, every single day, I looked forward in some vague way toward the next, toward the future, and found that what I looked at was opaque, that nothing was there, that I couldn't plan anything because no plan had meaning. While my son was alive, the future was assured, it was coming. If I died in the night, my plans would still in some sense go on, for my plans included security for a child, making his life possible.

The immediate purpose of a man's actions blinds him to the real meaning of them.

He saw the car from a distance. Dark blue. The correct numbers. Then he looked at the window. If the driver's window was closed, he was to walk by and go home. To return the next day at the same time. If it was open, he was to get in beside the driver and give the key phrase. In German and in English. He wondered why that was demanded.

The window was open. He glanced along the street. Was it safe? Who was to know? He climbed into the car and spoke the phrase. It was like a magician's spell. Now he was changed.

A man wishes to care for his family and knows instinctively that this is a right action, a moral action. But he cares for them, in most cases, by being party to the oppression of other men, other children. What happened to me was that suddenly, knowing myself as a childless man married to a woman who cared for nothing but what was dead, I could see clearly that there was no time to wait, that the future had lost its meaning for me unless I reached out and deliberately grasped a future that mattered. I became a political man. I once learned a little Greek tag, was it from Aristotle? That man is a political animal, although I was never sure that political was the right translation there. But it isn't all that inevitable. Man can remain outside any sense of community.

There are so many things to puzzle out. Who is my neighbour? That old question. What was the answer given? The parable of the good Samaritan, I think. But that leads no further than a soft charity. It was the eighteenth-century sentimental Christians who loved that parable. One good deed shining in a naughty world.

The Bible is full of beautiful questions. What shall I do to be saved? That's another good one. That's the one I was asking all those nights as I sat in my chair and stared at a book, feeling useless and helpless. I had always thought that what mattered was just to continue, to put one foot in front of the other.

I remember in university, I went through a period of depression. My father was still alive then, but so old and silent that he might as well have been dead. He had always been old, from my earliest memories of him, and we had always been, if not exactly poor in the sense that we went hungry, still poor enough that I seldom had more than two shirts at once and my mother worked as a daily cleaning woman at a couple of houses in town.

I was in the second year at university and still had made no real friends. The classes in history were huge, and the tutorials only occasional, and I couldn't make friends with anyone there. I had a couple of acquaintances, people who were as lonely as I was, but we had little in common, and the time we spent together seemed almost an embarrassment to us.

It was the time of the Korean War, I remember that very clearly. I couldn't afford to buy a newspaper, but sometimes I'd find one in Hart House or one of the classrooms. I always read the stories about the war first, without knowing why.

It was at that time that I convinced myself that all that mattered was to continue, even automatically, to go forward.

I remember I thought about my father's youth, the excitement of being in a revolution, at least until Kerensky was defeated. I'd learned about this only a couple of years before. He didn't like talking about the past, wouldn't even let me speak Russian or German if he could help it, but we were talking about Russia in school, and I asked him. I knew from my mother that he had been in fighting of some sort. When I asked him, he made a joke of the whole thing and said it didn't matter who won in any revolution, people would remain the fools they had always been.

Years later I discovered Trotsky's words to those like my father. *You are bankrupt. You have played out your role. Go where you belong: to the dustheap of history.*

The time of Korea: it took years, the clarification of issues, Guatemala, Cuba. Gradually, almost without my noticing, there grew in me the sense that the

American position was untenable. How would I have phrased it then? "They had certainly made mistakes, but they were our allies all the same." Stupid, stupid.

Men make their own history, but they do not make it just as they please. . . .

He stood in the dark street, shivering in the February cold that seemed to come through his heavy coat and invade the flesh. It was quiet now, and yet he could feel the life of Moscow taking place around him. An old woman opened the door of one of the houses and stared suspiciously at this man who stood in the middle of the street.

Could she read his thoughts? He imagined for a second that she could, that she could look at his face and recognize it as the face of a man who had decided to leave Russia, who had been walking the streets trying to make plans for his escape.

The old woman turned away and closed the door.

He didn't want to move, to walk. He had come into the narrow street almost deliberately, seeking dark, silence. Now he walked on, wondering if she watched him from behind. Since deciding to leave, he'd become self-conscious, as if the plan of flight must show in his face, as if the veins had become a map of his route.

Whether to leave or stay had been a terrible question, but finally it seemed clear that he must leave, that there was no place for him here. Where would he go? It hardly mattered. He had no goal except to leave behind what he couldn't like or understand. To run, perhaps that was it, but if so, yes, to run.

The accidents that changed me.

At the university I met Margaret when I was at the lowest point. We were both lonely, and we managed somehow to reach out together.

I sometimes wonder what Margaret's faith means to her now. What does God demand of her now that He's taken from her everything she cared for? Some kind of total humility? Faith? Faith in what? That somehow something will matter. Isn't that too nebulous? Perhaps she doesn't demand any more.

Other accidents too.

The death of the child.

The months in Bonn, because I happened to know German.

I knew, of course, why she was interested in me. We're warned about it, the guides that are too obliging, the women that bump against you in crowds. At first I didn't care.

I was coming back to life again. Perhaps that was it.

She was lying on her back, her eyes closed. A strange idea came to him, and he put his finger on her, just below her breasts, and began to trace letters down her belly. She opened her eyes and watched his face.

"What are you writing?" she said.

"F.R.E.E.D.O.M." he said.

It's a long time since I've had such a sense of controlled power. I am a human being again, although now I'm only waiting for instructions. Even the banality of my colleagues doesn't bother me. Now and then I meet people from the Eastern embassies. I find I'm avoiding them, wondering what they know. Nothing, I suppose, except for one or two. There must be great discipline in this work. That's a great part of its appeal. There's little in the way of a persuasive call to discipline in most lives. Duties are factitious and manufactured.

Should I be writing this at all? Perhaps not, but there's some kind of personal necessity in it. I am no good to them if I can't control and understand myself, and this journal is necessary if I am to have that understanding and control. As long as I keep it hidden. No-one but me has a key to the filing cabinet in our flat, and no-one has any reason to suspect that it contains anything of interest. I keep the book containing this journal at the back under a pile of old papers and diaries. Most of them are useless odds and ends that I saved in the belief that they might someday matter to someone, have some historical interest, or be useful if I ever decided to write a book.

Another of those hideous diplomat's memoirs.

Of course now that there is something worth writing, I can no longer hope to write it. Although Philby had it both ways. What if he had called his book *Memoirs of a Retired Civil Servant?*

I was thinking of Ottawa today, especially the time after the child died when the whole city seemed to have gone dead for us. It was the time of the Centennial celebrations, and I was kept running with arrangements for dignitaries to attend one thing or another. Then De Gaulle came, and the roof fell in.

Another great blow-up was the Cuban missile crisis. Everyone was convinced that Diefenbaker had lost his mind.

What did I really think then? The answer probably is that I didn't think at all, just assumed that I knew what it was all about and reacted like everyone else, but even then there was some part of my mind that was convinced that the Monroe Doctrine was nothing but an old and repeated threat, no better for the age and repetition. Especially when it was over and I started to look back at it, I began to wonder, but I still went on telling myself they were our allies, come what may. Freedom, the right to dissent, *etc, etc*.

Words, words, words. My folly, my total folly.

Only a fool can be a civil servant. No, not a fool, a hypocrite. Or a cynic. The job of the civil servant who has any judgment at all is to be paid for doing things that he thinks are wrong. When he agrees with policy, there's no problem, but he can't expect to agree with it more than half the time. That's the whole point of routine, to blind yourself to the dishonesty of what you're doing.

How I loved routine, too. I knew without being able to say it, that there was some kind of salvation in doing things correctly, that if I thought about the meaning of what I said or did, I'd go mad.

The other thing that saves us is the unimportance of most of what we do. There is so much busy-work, fiddling, that we forget that sometimes lives are at stake, that compromise is not right simply because it happens to be possible, that there are people who, when they have an opinion, state it. One of the reasons that civil servants hate politicians is that the politicians can sometimes say, even publicly, what they think.

The civil servant must obey his enemies.

She was not pretty, her motives were political, but she saved me. Accident again, that my frustration and confusion were at their peak when I met her.

Jim Allington is being sent over as my superior. All his plotting and planning are beginning to bear fruit. He is the archetypal ambitious civil servant, one third of his attention going on his job and two thirds on his ambitions. When we left Ottawa I was glad to be away from him, but I'm about to be faced with him again, this time as my superior officer. I'll have to defend and explain his stupid actions. That will give him pleasure, I'm sure. He'll do stupid things for the malicious pleasure of seeing me lumbered with their consequences. And all the time on the surface he'll be so pleasant. Little references to the fact that we're old friends, all meant to remind me that he has gone farther faster.

That's the kind of man I'm supposed to be loyal to. Being loyal to my country means being loyal to him. If anyone found out what I'm doing, there would be speeches about disloyalty, great clucking of tongues. Is the only possible loyalty loyalty to those who happen by chance to be close to you? Am I an evil man because I'm not loyal to Jim Allington? There's a phrase from Coke or one of the old jurists that I picked up somewhere. *Protection draws loyalty.* It sounds so simple like that, but protection from what draws what kind of loyalty? The state has not protected me from the sight of a world where airplanes drop fire on Vietnamese peasants, where so many people are hungry. What claims does it have on my loyalty?

The only real loyalty is loyalty to an idea, to the future, because the idea is always more perfect than any human embodiment. The future is perfect because it does not exist.

Future perfect: I will have acted correctly.

And what has Jim Allington ever protected me from? Someone worse? Impossible.

I watched Margaret tonight. Couldn't help myself, but went away and out for a walk. I found a store open and bought some candies. Thought of going to the movies but decided against it.

What does Margaret think? About me or anything? Sometimes at night I wake and look at her. I see her sleeping and wish I could look into her sleep.

Night walking. A time of secrets. Once or twice I have deliberately worked late, stayed at the office until everyone else has left and then gone through the building, trying doors, looking to see what I could find. Precious little, of course. They may have to wait a long time until I'm very useful to them. But they waited for Philby for nearly ten years.

All the secrets behind the drawn blinds of the houses. The middle class invented privacy and secrecy. Private property, closed doors. In England the brick walls in front of houses and between the yards, so openly hostile. In North America, there is more space, more chance to get a look at your neighbours, grassy playgrounds for envy, an affectation of openness with imprisoned minds buried behind laughing faces.

It's strange to realize that I own a house in Ottawa, on one of those leafy, expensive Rockcliffe streets. The flat here and my office contain all my new self. That house in Ottawa is where I lived in some previous life, when I was a different man.

It's very late now, but I don't want to go to bed. Tomorrow is Sunday, and I can sleep as late as I like. I'm beginning to wish that they'd get in touch with me. I must be patient until they're ready. But when I've committed myself to a course of action, it's not easy to see the action interrupted. I suppose it takes time to analyze what information they've got from me and decide how they should use me, what is most profitable for me to do.

Time is so slow tonight.

I got a letter from my young brother today. Sometimes I almost forget his existence. I still remember my shock when I was fifteen, and I discovered that my mother, who seemed to me an old woman, was pregnant. She never told me, and for a long time I thought she was sick. She was always tired, sometimes ate little, seemed generally distressed. It was many months before I discovered that she was pregnant, and the shock was not pleasant. I had always thought of my father as such an old man, so distant that it was almost impossible to imagine him as a sexual being. At first my mother seemed depressed by the pregnancy, but once the baby was born, she seemed younger and happier. I remember that I'd wake in the night and hear the baby crying, unable to think why there should be a baby crying in our house, then would realize that the anonymous baby was my brother Jacob.

I wonder what the old man thought about it. He always gave the impression that he didn't think at all about what happened in the house. He often had his meals alone in his little study and spoke to my mother only occasionally and nearly always in German or Russian. I learned German, but hardly any Russian, even my mother never spoke it, and when I'd see him in there reading old Russian books, it would seem to me that he belonged to a distant world in which I had no part.

The dustheap of history.

It pleased me to be able to tell the others in school that my father had been there in the Russian revolution, that he had really been there and seen it. They always asked if he was a communist. I'd explain that if he had been a communist, he wouldn't have left.

"Then what is he?" someone would say.

"Nothing," I'd say.

He's just an angry old man who hates everything, was what I wanted to say, but there was no use in getting into that.

Jacob must have been about five or six when he died. I was at university, my last year, I think. I remember that Margaret came to the funeral with me and how much my mother liked her. I only stayed a day or two, and I suppose I played with him a bit, but I have only a vague memory of a little boy who sat quietly at meals.

Since then I've seen him only occasionally when I've gone home to see my mother. Each time he's a surprise to me because he's grown and become a different person.

The letter I got today was once again a surprise. He seems to have become very political in a naive and idealistic way, like so many of his generation.

One can't be at ease with all one's allies.

I must answer the letter. In my pose as a mildly liberal, mildly conservative foreign service officer, I'll have to disagree with everything he says. Perhaps best just to argue the details of it with him.

It must have been odd for him growing up with no father and a mother so old, but I suppose it might be simpler to have no father than such a strange man as I was aware of. I must finish this and write to him.

What is the use of memory? Often as not it blinds us to the realities of the situation we are in. Do I need to look into my own past to understand or purify the present? Freudian nonsense. The past is dead. Nothing. Meaningless. What matters is the future. Let the dead bury their dead.

He saw a man staring at him in the Burlington Arcade. He thought it was the contact, but the man just walked away without speaking. He began to follow him.

We must be prepared to leave behind everything, the whole of history. To construct a new man and a new world. It's a terrifying thought so long as we cling to our small worlds, our bits of satisfaction, but as soon as we lay ourselves bare, the destruction of what we are or have ceases to matter, and we see only the brilliance of the future and ourselves as tools to be used by that future as it tries to come into existence. This is the only escape from inevitability, from the confusion of history. We can be free from history.

I was at a diplomatic reception this afternoon. There was a mild scandal. Someone's wife drank too much and fell the whole length of a staircase without doing herself any harm. I didn't see it myself but was told by one of the people from the FO.

Margaret manages amazingly well at such receptions. She says little, and when she does speak her stammer seems worse, but she smiles that gentle smile of hers, drinks nothing and carries it off beautifully. She makes everyone else around her seem shallow. As they are. What would have happened if the child hadn't died?

Never answer hypothetical questions.

There's been a long pause in this. I've been very busy and also nervous because they hadn't made contact with me, but the contact came today. A letter arrived with the mail. It was from a theatre, and inside was one ticket. At first I thought it must be a mistake, but then I realized what it was. The ticket is for this Thursday week. All there is for me to do now is wait and go to the play that night. I wonder how they'll make the contact?

I feel better now that something is underway. I'd begun to think that I was almost my old self again. Yesterday I was wandering around Mayfair and saw a couple of military prints in the window of a bookshop, uniforms from the Napoleonic wars. I looked at them for a few minutes, tempted to buy them but thinking that I'd given up such things. But then I thought that I must maintain my old self, at least publicly, and I went in and got them.

This afternoon I wrote a good analysis of the British attitude to our role in NATO and NORAD. I'd got some useful ideas at the reception the other day. I spent some time talking to a very intelligent Greek. I couldn't make out just how he felt about the colonels, but he had some good ideas about NATO.

Margaret is sick in bed with some kind of heavy cold

or flu. I offered to stay home, but she said she'd phone Mrs. Taverner if she needed anything. The doctor is coming round later this evening.

I suppose it's the heavy rain of the last few days. She must have got a chill.

Why is it that I think of her as so much older than I am? I suppose because she's ended up being like my mother when I was home, just silently there, providing me with food and a pleasant place to live, but not much involved in anything that happens. I have to remind myself that Margaret is exactly my age, not fifteen years older. Many times after the death of the child I made some kind of sexual overture toward her, but it was clear that she was revolted, and I gave it up.

I suppose our relationship with each other was always more protective than passionate. We met when we were at university, both lonely, and we began to spend a great deal of time together, studying, walking, going to concerts. I started to take some English courses that we could take together so we could have that much more in common.

She was allowed to have a dinner guest at her residence occasionally and would take me, once a month or so, to have dinner there. I always found it embarrassing eating with all those girls and trying to make conversation but the food was a change from what I cooked myself.

That was the first year we met, my second year at university. I got a good summer job that year through Margaret's father, and the next year I lived in one of the residence houses. That made life a lot simpler.

We didn't sleep together until we were married. That was just after I'd been accepted into External. Margaret's religious feelings were so strong that I couldn't imagine trying to change them. I always felt the need to be very gentle and protective with her, and I found that satisfying. It seemed that some whole new

68

part of me had awakened, and while I was aware of having to control my desire, it was possible, even easy, because of this protective feeling. But somehow after the death of the child she no longer needed or wanted that protection. She just left me behind when she went down into herself. When that happened, the whole sexual frustration came to the surface.

I need more control.

I am a fool perhaps, but there is something, almost courage, in my ordinariness, my folly.

Jim Allington has arrived, full of self-congratulatory smiles, of course, careful to mention that he hasn't seen me for two years (not mentioning the promotion). There was a moment when I really wanted to say "Yes, Jim, I'm fine. I've become a spy." I don't suppose he ever listens. He'd have shaken my hand and said he was glad to hear it. I really have no idea why anyone should promote him to any position. I suppose I do really. He's plausible, and he devotes himself to seeing the right people and saying the right things. He may be useful to me. Sometimes he provokes people to say more than they intend to, and the information could be valuable. I have the theatre ticket and am planning to go, but I sometimes wonder how much more I have to offer. It sometimes seems to me that I've passed on much of what I know already. Still it would be amusing if Jim either gave me or caused someone else to give me information that I could usefully pass on. I've made a few notes about what I've picked up on recent troop dispositions in Europe, but it isn't much. Perhaps I could use a camera. I'm not sure.

Margaret is much better today. I've been worried about her. We have little contact except for superficial things, but I still have a sense of loyalty to her. What strange fantasies go through my head about her sometimes.

Is any man ever satisfied? Imagination and consciousness are a terrible burden. I can imagine so much. Is it possible to control this? It's supposed to be.

Three more days until the meeting.

Allington has crashed into our conferences with the full resources of vulgarity and stupidity he has at his disposal. It really does make me shudder to watch him in action. I'll get used to it again but these things take time. (That sounds like an expression that he'd use. He's everywhere.) Still I think he's led me to some interesting things. He's a first-class snoop. Too bad I can't recruit him. He's almost venal enough to be bought. Why bother with him?

I've had another letter from my brother, answering all the things I said in my letter. There's something touching about his seriousness. Will he and his generation change the world? Of course. Every generation does, one way or another. But they want to start everything anew, not to trust anyone at all. You must start somewhere. That's what I have done. Nothing is perfect, but we must choose a place to start within history and follow it into the future. He wants to deny history.

The meeting is tomorrow night. I find myself wondering why they chose a theatre. How can we talk in such a crowd?

8

Jake came out of the tube station and looked around him, annoyed with himself for taking the wrong train and coming by the longest route. Now there wasn't much time left before he was due at Canada House. He looked around him. To his left and overhead was the cement overpass of a motorway, not yet opened, and across the road in front of one of the concrete supports was a big sign. He crossed over and read it. It said *Your Social Rights and Information Centre here soon.* Underneath was a plan of the centre that was to be built under the motorway. It looked great, but Jake was skeptical.

As he stood there on the cinders he looked at a slogan written across the wall beside him in yellow paint.

MAY 13
WHERE WAS I AT THIS TIME LAST YEAR?
ON THE BARRICADES IN PARIS.

It made him think of Member. It was only a few more days until the Action Group would be holding their demonstration. In a way Jake wished he could be there.

He'd made himself a little map from a street guide so he could find his way to Don Hattersley's, but he didn't bother getting it out yet. He wanted to wander for a while. As he walked, he looked at the houses around him, sure that all this was rented housing broken into little bits and pieces to make the highest possible profit. You could tell to look at the buildings.

Jake bought a couple of apples from a barrow beside the road. He hadn't eaten since breakfast, and he'd started to get a bit hungry but didn't feel like stopping for a proper lunch.

As he turned a corner, he could hear the noise of children playing in a schoolyard, but they were behind a high brick wall, and he couldn't see them. He saw a familiar name on a street he was passing, took out his map and discovered that the street he was looking for was close by, and when he had found it, it was only a few houses to the address he'd been given.

On the street outside the house, someone had been dismantling a car for the parts, and a chunk of the driveshaft lay on the sidewalk. When Jake got to the door, he found there was a single doorbell that looked as if it hadn't worked for quite a while. He knocked loudly on the door and waited. Nothing happened.

Jake knocked again, even louder this time, and after a moment he heard noises inside. An old man opened the door. He was wearing a torn cardigan and baggy trousers, but the thing that struck Jake as he looked at him was the strange look of his skin, almost as if it were transparent.

"I'm looking for Don Hattersley. He's an American."

"Oh, he's gone. Lived right in here, this front room."

"Do you know where he's gone to?"

"Not far. I've seen him about. You ask at the shop on the corner. They'll tell you."

"Thanks."

The old man closed the door. Jake wondered whether there was any point asking at the store. He decided there was nothing to lose. As he walked toward the store, he saw a poster advertising a meeting about housing. He read the little parody in the centre of it.

Our Council which art in Heaven,
Hallowed be thy name,
Thy Kensington come
Thy people be done. . . .

When he walked into the store, a man came from the back to serve him.

"I'm looking for Don Hattersley, an American. Someone told me you might know where to find him."

"Second house from the end on the other side. In the basement."

Jake thanked the man and walked down the street toward the tubular steel scaffolding where the concrete supports for the motorway were being built. He went down the steep steps to the basement area and knocked on the door.

It was opened by a man who was taller than Jake, maybe a little older. He had a blond moustache and striking, almost frightening, blue eyes.

"I'm looking for Don Hattersley." Jake said.

"That's me."

"I got your name from Al Sturgess."

"Come in."

He made room for Jake to pass by. They walked into a large room with a bed on one side, a table and a couple of straight chairs on the other, and a great pile of odds and ends and extra chairs in the middle that made it hard to move around. A girl with long dark hair was sitting on the bed and a young man who appeared to be an Indian or Pakistani stood in the middle of the room. There were posters and revolutionary slogans on most of the walls. In front of Jake was one that said HE WHO WATCHES A CRIME IN SILENCE COMMITS IT.

"This is Lucy," Hattersley said, indicating the girl on the bed, "and this is Rafiq."

"I'm Jake Martens."

Rafiq put out his hand and Jake shook it. The man

had fine and very even features. He was wearing an elegant tweed suit that looked out of place in the untidy room.

"I really must be off now," Rafiq said. "I've stayed too long already."

"You're definitely going back?" Hattersley said.

"Yes. I must. I ran away from Karachi because I couldn't stand watching all my rich relatives trying to imitate bad Hollywood movies while people starved. I thought I'd come back to England and be happy and useful. But I'm only fooling myself, aren't I? I must go back to my people. Pakistan is terrible, truly terrible, but I belong there."

"You can be useful here," Hattersley said.

"No, I belong there. They are my people. But I'll be in touch before I go."

He walked to the door.

"It's very nice to have met you," he said to Jake. "Goodbye now." He went out and closed the door behind him. Hattersley turned back to Jake, who was still standing in the middle of the room.

"Sit down," he said. "What brings you over?"

"You wouldn't believe it."

"Some kind of secret?"

"Did you read in the papers about a spy in the Canadian diplomatic service?"

Hattersley nodded.

"My brother," Jake said.

The man nodded again.

"I came to try and find out what's going on. For my old lady."

"Will they tell you anything?"

"I don't know. I've got to see somebody this afternoon."

"They won't tell you anything. They're all fucking paranoid."

"Could be."

"What's Al doing anyway? Is there any protest movement in Canada?"

"That's how I met him."

"Shit, the thing's completely international, isn't it? I've met people here from France, Sweden, Czechoslovakia, Rafiq and his friends from Pakistan, and we're all fighting the same war. It's a real indigenous international movement."

Jake nodded.

"How long have you been here?" the other man said.

"Just since yesterday. I got lost on the tube this morning."

"You should try to stay for a while. There are some really good things happening. The housing situation around here is unbelievable, you must have seen this district. And there isn't even enough of this. The Kensington Council just wants to push all these people out so they can have a nice tidy middle-class community. There's no fucking place for people to go except lousy hostels. But some militant squatters' groups have got going. There must be three or four in London."

"Just move people into empty houses?"

"Yeah. At home they'd be shot down in the streets, but they can do it here. They really can. Shit, even if the people only get two or three months in the place, they're that much better off. It's one more step. You know what some people left behind when they got thrown out of one place? A great big sign, 'We are the writing on your wall.'"

"How did you end up in England?" Jake said.

"I came here to study, but I gave it up. I decided there were more important ways to spend my time. I may go home in a few months. I've overstayed my visa so it'll be sooner than that if they catch me. But I don't think it matters where you are. It's the same revolution everywhere."

The girl got up from the bed and walked toward

75

the gas ring, where a kettle was starting to boil.

"Anybody want coffee?" she said. Jake was surprised to hear another American accent.

"I wouldn't mind some coffee," he said.

"Me too," Hattersley said. He turned back to Jake. "We've got some people moving into an empty place tomorrow, right near here. Why don't you come and help? The more people we've got, the faster we can get them in."

The girl came and handed them each a cup of coffee. She passed a bowl of sugar and a grubby pint of milk and handed over the spoon she was using. Jake liked the feel of the cup of coffee warm in his hands.

Someone knocked at the door of the room.

"Come on in," Hattersley said.

Jake turned toward the door and saw a slogan written on the wall beside it. WE ARE ALL CONSPIRATORS. The door opened and a heavy-set wide-faced man came in.

"Tom," Hattersley said, "how's everything? Is it all set?"

"I've got hold of a van to take their gear," he said.

"Jake here is going to help us move the stuff."

"Another American?" the man said looking at Jake.

"Canadian," Hattersley said.

"All the same, isn't it?" the man said.

"There's about ten thousand draft dodgers who'll tell you it isn't," Hattersley said.

The man came over to Jake and put out his hand.

"Tom Walsh," he said.

"I'm Jake Martens."

"His brother's a spy," Hattersley said.

"Is that the bloke that's in all the papers?" Tom Walsh said. Jake nodded.

"They'll be wanting to put you on the telly," he said.

"Not if I can help it," Jake said.

"Christ, the papers would give you a few quid. Not

76

what you'd get for having it off with Barbara Castle and telling about it, but you can't be too fussy."

He sat down on the bed beside Lucy. She moved over to make room for him.

"What time do we go tomorrow?" Hattersley said.

"I'm getting the van around ten, but I won't be able to bring it round here till ten-thirty anyway. Say I meet you here by eleven." He turned to Jake. "Are you coming?"

"If you want some extra help, sure."

Tom Walsh nodded. As he sat there on the low bed, his heavy sweater was bulky around him, and in the poor light he looked like some kind of dwarf, as wide as he was tall. Jake looked at his watch and stood up. It was after one o'clock.

"I better get going," he said. "I've got to be at Canada House at two. See if they'll tell me anything."

"Not a chance," Hattersley said. "Not in the interests of national security."

"Tomorrow at eleven then," Tom Walsh said.

"I'll be here," Jake said and walked out. He took what seemed the shortest way to a tube station, remembering what Don Hattersley had told him about the squatters. It was so simple and right.

9

I arrived at the theatre early. Most of the seats around me were empty at first, and as they filled up, I found myself watching everyone, as unobtrusively as I could, and wondering what would happen. I was shaking. I mentally made fun of myself for being so nervous, but that didn't stop the way I was feeling. There was a very pretty girl sitting just in front of me, and she distracted me for a few minutes. Then I read the program, word by word, even the advertisements. It was nearly time for the curtain when someone sat down beside me. The seat on the other side was still empty. I thought this must be Simon, but he paid no attention to me. The play began with me half watching, half speculating on the reason for the empty seat. The jokes did not strike me as funny, but I was preoccupied. Nothing happened for most of the first act, but just before the intermission, the man beside me dropped his program into my lap. I looked toward him, but he did not look my way, so I kept the program and watched the rest of the act. As soon as the lights went on, he got up from his seat and left, going out the other way so that he didn't pass me. I looked down at the program, which seemed to have something inside it, and then put it in the inside pocket of my coat and went out to the lobby. There was no sign of the man who had sat beside me, and I marvelled at how smoothly he had managed the whole thing. I wanted to leave and look at the program, but I thought it was safer to stay till the end.

When I did leave, I went to my car and drove home before looking at the program I'd been given. Margaret was in bed asleep, so I went into the study and set it down on the desk. Inside the program I found part of a map of Kew Gardens. On one of the walks was written *An excellent view of the river. Especially at high tide.* I looked the map over carefully. There was nothing else written or marked on it. I was puzzled and it was several minutes before I had the sense to look through the rest of the program. When I finally did, I found near the back, in a listing of exhibitions, a date and time had been circled. Next Wednesday at three o'clock.

I find myself now trying to remember the man who sat beside me. I only glanced at him once or twice after the house lights had gone down, and my impression is simply of a European, something about his face suggested that, somewhat heavy-set, with glasses. That's really all I can remember about him.

I must make sure that I am clear next Wednesday afternoon. I suppose the simplest thing is not to come back after lunch. Let Jim Allington take care of things on his own.

Margaret seems to be getting sick again. She went to bed right after dinner tonight.

When the doctor came, he said there was nothing serious wrong with her, but I don't trust him entirely. He seemed so cheerful and offhand about everything.

I'd like to talk to Margaret and make her understand how this has brought me back to life. What she needs is something to commit herself to. I once mentioned adopting a child, but she seemed to find the idea horrifying. I'd mention it again, but I no longer have the freedom to commit myself to a child.

I've been glancing at Guevara's book on the revolutionary war in Cuba. Hard to follow in ways. It's never clear to me just how things happened, but I suppose that's always true of anything that's close to the documentary reality. As soon as you move in close, you get a Tolstoyan view of history, a multiplicity of motives, and events that happen strangely, almost providentially. Tolstoy saw the foolishness of believing that great men make history, but never saw the rest.

Freedom is being at one with history.

The meeting is tomorrow. I've made a summary of what I know about NATO and NORAD planning at the moment and will take that with me. It seems pitifully little, and I can't believe they don't know it already, but it is the kind of information we would normally keep locked in a security file, so perhaps it really is secret.

I've finally met him. I had a sandwich in a pub at lunch time and then walked down to the Charing Cross tube station. I'd accidentally met Geoffrey Bailey in the pub, and I was afraid I'd have to make explanations, but he was rushing off somewhere, so there was no need. I'd thought of taking my car or a cab out to Kew Gardens, but somehow it seemed safer to take the tube. Now I'm not sure I was right. I felt exposed as I sat there for the long tube ride out, as if everyone who got on the car looked at me and wondered why I was there. The ride seemed endless.

I'd only been there once before and that time by car, so I'd checked in the street guide to make sure I knew the way from the station, but I still managed to get lost and had to ask my way in a candy store. I suppose I can rely on the fact that hundreds of people every year have to ask the way. Still he would notice my accent.

It was a quarter of a mile or so to the gates of the gardens, and quite a long way through the gardens to the riverside where I was to meet him. I checked my watch and discovered that I'd be a few minutes early, but I had brought a newspaper to read which would keep me from looking too much out of place while I waited.

When I got to the riverside, I didn't realize at first that I was there. I was surprised at how narrow the river is there, especially when the tide it out, as it was this afternoon. There was a bench overlooking the river at about the correct spot, but when I arrived, there was an old man sitting on it. I wondered if he could be the contact, but decided that it was impossible.

It was only ten to three, so I walked along the path nearest the river, trying to give the impression that I was just enjoying the gardens and strolling at my ease. I've never been less at ease in my life. Now and then I looked back, and finally I saw the old man get off the bench and move away. I turned and went back.

When I was settled with my paper, I felt a little more relaxed. This was how I had rehearsed the whole thing in my mind, and I preferred to have it fit my plans.

A woman walked in front of me, along the fence that separates the gardens from the riverside. She looked at me, and for a moment, I wondered if Simon could be a woman. I knew it was impossible, for she was old and very British looking, but I watched her as she walked under the trees.

There was a man sitting on the bench beside me. It sounds strange to put it that way, but I swear I didn't hear or see him come. I suppose I was paying so much attention to the woman that I didn't hear him come from behind.

"An excellent view of the river," he said.

I nodded.

"Especially at high tide," I said.

I looked around. There was no-one near.

"You must be Simon," I said.

He suggested that we walk along the grass near the river. It took me a minute or so to get used to his presence. He was not the same man who had sat beside me at the play. This man was taller, better dressed. He wasn't somehow quite what I had expected. We talked as we moved through the gardens. He kept glancing nervously around us, to see that we didn't come too close to anyone else in the park, but there were few people there. It was a relief in a way to be with him because I knew that I must trust him, let him be in control.

He asked me whether I needed money. I said not. He seemed quite anxious to give me some. I told him that I knew why he was offering the money, that I didn't want it, and that he didn't need any kind of stick to hold over me. I was angry because I had felt that I could trust him and now, it seemed to me, he wasn't returning my trust. He apologized. I had the feeling that this was some kind of test, to see how clear my motives were.

I told him that I had some material for him and gave him the notes that I had prepared. He glanced through them and complimented me on the brevity and clarity of the statement. He said it would be very useful. It was then I mentioned a couple of things that Allington has let slip, just suggestions that I can't entirely explain. He was interested, but he started to question me about Jim Allington and what he'd been doing in Ottawa. He asked a lot of detailed questions. I told him as much as I could. Found myself analyzing things that had happened years before. I got a strange feeling about it, partly because it seemed to me that he might be remembering everything I said. I have a good memory for detail, but I couldn't have mastered so much information so fast. Perhaps he wasn't, but it seemed to me that he was. I was exhausted after trying to answer all his questions. We had walked to the far end of the Gardens and turned back the way we'd come by this time.

Then he began to discuss procedures. He gave me an address in the East End. In case of emergency, I'm to mail an empty blue envelope to that address and wait for them to contact me.

If they ever need to contact me by phone, there will first be a call asking for James and apologizing for calling a wrong number. They will claim to have called a number two digits different from mine. If I can accept their call, I will tell them my own number.

If not, I will simply say that they have called the wrong number.

We arranged another meeting in three weeks at a place near the edge of Epping Forest.

After we'd finished, he went back toward the main gate and told me to leave by the gate where I'd come in. I had some trouble finding my way through the twisting paths and didn't dare ask anyone, so by the time I found the gate and got back on the train, I was exhausted. Once there I felt once again that I was being looked at. I became very depressed, partly, I think, because I was so tired. It seemed to me that Simon didn't trust me and that he would inevitably be disappointed in what I had to offer.

Whenever I get depressed there is a strange sexual excitement that goes along with it, a febrile, unhealthy thing. I could feel that growing in me as I sat there on the train and watched a girl farther down the aisle.

When I got back to the office, I found Jim Allington looking for me. It wasn't hard to make an excuse, but it was one more irritation that I had to cope with him.

Driving home, I had a foul headache and found myself furiously angry at the traffic and myself, at everything that had happened. When I got home, I told Margaret that I didn't feel well. I went to bed where I managed to sleep for a couple of hours in spite of the headache and depression. When I woke, I was hungry, and after I had eaten, I sat down to think for a few minutes. I was much calmer and found that I could see the whole thing more clearly. It was very arrogant of me to assume that Simon would immediately trust me. I've said that all I want is to be used, and if I accept that and stay with it, then I must realize that I am only one small source of information, that the little I can give must be put together with the little that others can give. Only when they are added together can they amount to anything important. When I had sorted this out, I felt much better and sat down to write.

Today is Sunday. This afternoon I drove south of the river through parts of the city I'd never seen before, some of the working-class areas. The strongest impression the people give is of hostility, although it's odd how they pick the objects of their dislike. I stopped to buy a package of mints, and the reaction to my accent was obvious. I was an American, and Americans are the enemy. Is it too hard to hate a system? Must emotions always be personalized in this way? I notice that the communist labour leaders here are distinguished not by hope or any sense of the future, but by their more intense hatreds.

He knows that those he meets are contacts, are important to him, but cannot remember which are his friends, which his enemies.

He stared at the man who sat across from him, trying to find something in the features of the face that would tell him what he should feel. It was a round face, at first a friendly face, but there was something, perhaps that fact that one eye was larger than the other. . . . There was a small wart on the side of his face. He looked again. The man smiled.

Was the smile a prelude to an action? An attack? It was clear that the man was important to him, was an essential contact, or perhaps an enemy, the man he most had to fear.

He tried to use the image of a book, his recollections the writing in the book, but when he opened the book, there were only blank pages. So once again he looked back at the man and tried to read his features, to find the source of the familiarity. For a moment he was prepared to think that the whole thing was an elaborate hoax, that someone had composed the face from various features that were familiar to him.

Every word the man spoke was seized on, searched, backed against the walls of his brain to test it. What were they supposed to be discussing? The ostensible subjects, the restaurant, the weather, were so clearly nothing—only hints.

Did this man know what had happened to his memory? He no longer dared to look up and see the face.

Worse still, was he responsible? Had they done something to him? Could this conversation be a test of their success?

It came to him that this amnesia was very strange, for the world was not new, not altogether new. His mind was not that of a newborn child. The forgetting was selective, and there were feelings, intuitions that functioned even though he couldn't explain them.

He looked back up at the man who, absurdly, winked at him. He smiled.

They had made some kind of deal, some kind of bond. It was settled now that the round face was to be known to him.

Without knowing this man, without knowing even his own name any more, he had chosen sides. Was he right or wrong—in the sense of the past—was this the same side or a new one? Not that it mattered now. It was done.

There has been a pause of two weeks in this. I've received the camera, an Exacta, and have spent some time mastering it. I got a couple of books about photography, and I think by now I understand it and can use it efficiently. I keep it locked in my filing cabinet along with a strong bulb that makes it easier to photograph documents. I have an address where I'm to send the undeveloped films, not the same as the emergency address.

The whole thing strikes me as so very strange, the latent image produced on the film in some fraction of a second, an image that can be destroyed by exposure to light or developed and made permanent by some kind of chemicals. I'll never know how my pictures come out. No doubt they'll tell me if they're disastrously bad.

The delivery of the camera: I received an envelope containing a key for a left luggage locker in Victoria Station. The camera was in the locker. I could simply have bought one, of course. They must know best. They've been in the business longer than I have.

I find there is a remarkable fascination to working on two levels of the mind at the same time, being two people at once. Often I find that I am participating in a conversation that is meant to go somewhere and sort out a certain series of ideas, while at the same time, I'm planning how to obtain information about related subjects. It's an intriguing situation. I have a constant double awareness, as in certain kinds of comedy. That is the effect, to make everything somewhat comical because of the detachment.

Philby must have had an extreme and delightful awareness of this sort. I should think the one pleasure of being a double agent is this exaggerated awareness of the discrepancy between the real and the apparent. Every intelligent person knows that the real is deceptive, that there may be many realities and that some contradict others, but the secret agent lives the contradiction, and the double agent is totally immersed in it. I suppose that is the fascination of shoddy spy fiction for a society where everyone is aware that he is playing a part in a great charade, where duty has no purchase on the soul, that the spy is our fantasy of a controlled impersonation, a conscious use of the masks we all wear.

I met Simon again two days ago. He wanted to know about the organization of our people here in great detail, especially the military people and anyone who had contact with the Americans. I couldn't give him all the information he wanted. The Defence people at Grosvenor Square don't broadcast what they're doing, but I told him what I could. He wanted to know about personalities, anyone he might recruit, and I got the impression again that I don't have all the access he wants. I said this, but he insisted that they were very satisfied with what I was doing, that his superiors had mentioned my material very favourably, but that he needed supplementary information to go with it. When he had explained this, he started to go back over what I'd given him, checking some points and asking for amplification of others. I find myself engaging in little contests with him, trying to guess what points he'll want to know more about or guessing where he may have made mistakes. He does get things wrong, of course. Anyone would, but his average is pretty high. From our conversation, he worked out a couple of areas where he wants information that I can get, more or less legitimately, but it is material I must photograph since he wants it all in written form.

Our next meeting is at Kew Gardens again.

When I got back to the office, I thought at first that Jim Allington might be suspicious about my excuse, but I suppose he was just being difficult for its own sake. How I dislike that man.

Once again after this meeting, I found that I was exhilarated only for a few moments and then suddenly depressed. It was less severe this time, but still not easy to deal with. I went to bed early when I got home.

I brought home some documents and photographed them tonight. I find it hard to believe they are safely recorded on that film and won't come to be destroyed somehow or turn out to be badly exposed. I've never had this strange feeling about a camera before, the few times I've used one, but I suppose it's the importance of this that suddenly makes me aware of the mystery of the whole process. I hope that I can return these things safely. One or two of them are from general files, and I'd find it hard to explain why I had them home. I think these could be very important.

I got the files back safely. One of the girls was being very friendly today, almost flirtatious. Very tempting, but the thought of carrying on some kind of secret affair is just too much on top of the rest of the secrecy. She would demand some kind of emotional involvement that just isn't in me to give. If she'd been around a few months ago, I suppose everything might have been different.

Am I that much a slave of circumstances?

I just thought of the Latin root of circumstance and had a vision of circumstances as a group of young men *standing around*, waiting for something to happen, or for someone to react to them. Like the adolescent boys who stand around on the streets at night, just waiting, not for anything in particular, just waiting.

I have some papers locked in my desk that I couldn't get home today. Jim Allington came into my office just as I was about to leave and asked me for a ride home. I couldn't refuse and didn't feel like taking them out while he was there. So they are locked in my desk, useless.

I've become fascinated with papers. Something else that I've never really thought about before. What would we do if there was no paper? Would we be worse off? Here I am committing myself to a certain kind of action, a certain kind of change, and my use is in making copies of papers and passing them on to other people who will make more copies, then clip on memos and put them in files with other papers. I suppose that's why young men like my brother are so committed to actions, to marching and shouting. Their word activist. But activity, movement for its own sake, will create chaos. The paper is an attempt to create a pattern for the movement, but it can become an impediment.

What do the papers contain, really? A pattern for planned activity, the future. To act and to plan to act. Tomorrow I will go to the office. If I am still alive tomorrow I will go to the office. I will go to the office if I care to. The statistical probability is that I will go to the office.

Tomorrow I will change the world.

I could plan that, of course, but the plan would not mean anything. But to say that I will go to the office tomorrow is just to assume a repetition of the past. What is the point of the future if it is not freedom? Yesterday I changed the world. That's a lie, well, perhaps not in the sense that any action changes some other, *etc*. Yesterday I ate a pork pie for lunch. That is a lie. Tomorrow I will eat a pork pie for lunch. Not yet a lie, though I hate pork pie and am not likely to be eating one.

Where can I find the future? Or have I found it?

I'd better go to bed.

10

As Jake walked toward Canada House, he was struck by the size of the building, and he wondered who had built it, the Canadian government or one of the English aristocrats who had once been able to afford this kind of place.

He turned and looked across Trafalgar Square before walking in. It looked just like all the postcards. He'd been meaning to buy some postcards and send them, especially one for his mother, as if that would somehow reassure her that she was getting her money's worth out of the trip.

He turned to the pillared doorway and walked in. Toward the back of the big hallway was a receptionist. Jake walked up to her.

"I've got an appointment with somebody named Allington."

She gave him an odd look, as if Allington wasn't in the habit of seeing people in boots and jeans.

"What's your name, please?"

"Jake Martens."

She looked at some kind of list on her desk, picked up the phone and dialed.

"Mr. Allington? Mr. Martens is here. Yes, that's fine."

"There's an elevator over there," she said. "Go up to the second floor."

Jake went to the elevator. When he got out at the second floor, there was an elderly Englishman in a sort of butler's uniform standing nearby.

"Did you have an appointment with someone?" he said.

"Yeah," Jake said, "a man named Allington."

"Just come this way, sir."

They had gone a few feet down the hall when they were met by a large smooth-haired man in a grey suit.

"Mr. Allington," the old man said, "this gentleman says he has an appointment with you."

"Oh yes," the other man said, "you're Mr. Martens."

Jake nodded. The place was beginning to get on his nerves. The old man left them, and Allington led him to an office nearby. It had a door into the hall, and another door into the secretary's office beside it where two girls were typing. When they got into the office, Allington motioned Jake to a chair and closed both doors. As he was closing the door to the secretary's office, Jake heard one of the girls ask him if he wanted her to make some tea.

"I don't think so," he said, closed the door and sat down behind the desk.

"Now before we start," he said, giving Jake a sombre look, "I'm afraid I'll have to ask you for some kind of identification. You can imagine what kind of a time we've had with the newspapers on this business, and it's not beyond some of them to find out that John Martens had a brother and send someone round here to impersonate him."

Jake took the wallet out of his back pocket and threw it on the desk. For a second, Allington looked as if he'd refuse to touch it, but he opened it for a second, glanced at something and pushed it away across the desk. Jake didn't bother picking it up.

"Well now," Allington said, "just what is it you want to know?"

"I want to know what's happened to my brother."

"So do we. I'd be glad to know that myself."

He looked at Jake and said nothing.

"Look," Jake said, "my mother's an old woman. She knows nothing about politics. She doesn't even speak English too well. Some mountie who's been trained to stand at attention on Parliament Hill and bully a few Indians and Eskimos. . . ." Allington interrupted him.

"That's not really very fair now, is it?"

"OK, so he's also been trained to bust someone on a drug beef now and then, but anyway. . . ."

"I don't think I like your attitude," Allington said.

"I don't think I asked you to like it," Jake said.

Allington's face started to get pale. Jake got the impression that the smooth hair had just separated itself from the scalp beneath and was living an independent life.

"Listen to me," Allington said. "I don't have to answer any questions of yours at all. This is just a courtesy I'm offering you, and I don't have to stand any cheek."

"No, you sure don't," Jake said, "but how would you like me to walk straight out of here and into a newspaper office to tell them that I've come all the way from Canada to try to get some information for my mother about her eldest son, and that the nice people at Canada House had something to hide and told me to fuck off."

"I'm not impressed," Allington said.

Jake reached for his wallet and stood up.

"OK," he said, "thanks a lot."

As he turned away, he heard the man stand up.

"Just a minute now, Martens. Let's just approach this calmly for a minute."

"Fine with me," Jake said.

They were both standing.

"Sit down," Allington said.

Jake went back to the chair. Allington took his place behind the desk.

"Now I know," Allington said, "in a situation like this, feelings run high, and no-one is quite as calm as they should be. . . ."

This time it was Jake's turn to interrupt.

"Look," he said, "you don't like me, and I don't like you. Nothing's going to change that, but we've got this thing we should talk about. You pretend I'm not really here, and I'll pretend you're not really here, and we'll try to get it over with."

"All right," Allington said. He was still furious, but contained now.

"The mountie," Jake said, "who was a fine upstanding citizen of Canada. . . ." Allington looked

92

toward him. "Relax," Jake said. "This mountie told my mother a story like the one they told me. About how my brother had disappeared, and they thought he'd been spying, and if he turned up he'd be arrested."

Allington nodded.

"My mother's an old woman, and she lives all by herself and knows nothing about spies, and she phoned me because the beautiful mountie's beautiful story upset her a little. She wanted me to come to England to find out something for her, so I came."

"Have you seen the newspapers?"

"The Canadian ones."

"There really isn't much more to tell than they had."

"Maybe you could try."

"I came here late in June to take charge of our section dealing with military affairs between us and Britain. There's a very close relationship between our armed forces and the British forces, but there are political aspects of our military affairs, NATO for example, that cause us to get involved. That's what I was sent to supervise. The people in Ottawa wanted someone here who was up-to-date on our thinking during a touchy period. I was senior to your brother, although we worked co-operatively, of course.

"When I got here, I thought right away that John was. . . well, he was a little strange. He'd always kept a bit apart, even when I'd known him in Ottawa." He stopped.

Jake sat and waited.

"Have you talked to Margaret about it?" Allington said.

Jake nodded.

"Well, then, you really must know all there is to know. He didn't show up for work one morning. Margaret phoned to say he hadn't been home the previous night. We phoned the police right away, but it wasn't until later that day that we got a call from the hostel saying someone had left a briefcase, and they'd looked in it and found that he'd worked here."

"Margaret said he'd written some kind of journal."

"That's right."

"Where is it?"

"The police have it."

"Have you seen it?"

Allington hesitated before he answered.

"Yes," he said.

"I'd like to see it."

"That would be quite impossible."

"Why?"

"It's a security matter. We couldn't let it be made public."

"Sweep everything under the rug."

"Surely you understand, in the circumstances. . . ."

"What circumstances?"

"The police are involved in an investigation concerning the national security of Canada and Great Britain, and it isn't possible to tell the whole world what's involved. Can't you understand that?"

"I don't believe in obscure ideas like 'national security,' and I don't believe in the need for secret conspiracies to suppress evidence, but I don't expect you to agree with me."

"I'm glad."

"When you came here and thought he was behaving in a strange way, did you tell anyone about it?"

"I can't tell you that."

"Did he know you suspected him?"

"I'd have no way of knowing that, would I?"

"Do the police know where he is?"

"I don't think so."

"Do you think he's alive?"

"He apparently walked out of the hostel early last Thursday morning. Nobody seems to have seen him

since. You must know about Burgess and Maclean
and Philby."

"I know the names."

"They all disappeared and turned up later in
Moscow. Maybe the same thing will happen with
your brother. Six months or a year from now some
journalist in Moscow may spot him on the street. Who
knows? Once a man decides to betray his country,
it's hard to predict what he'll do. Maybe you wouldn't
understand that."

"Maybe I wouldn't. I don't think you're the man
I want to discuss it with."

"Just as well."

"This journal, it can't all be about spying."

"No, not really. Just a kind of psychological garbage
can in a way. Heaven knows why he wrote it. It was
very foolish. The people he was working for will be
very upset if they find out about it. I hope they do.
That's what he deserves."

"You have a talent for unpleasantness, don't you?"

"It probably depends on the company I'm in."

"Can I see some of the parts that won't make me a
security risk?"

"I don't think so."

"Why not?"

"What purpose would it serve?"

"It might help me explain things to my mother."

"I doubt it. It's a nasty little document really, and
practically everything in it is better allowed to die.
I think I can assure you that if your brother were to
express his opinion, he'd want to have it destroyed."

"But I've only got your word for that."

"That's right. You'll just have to trust me."

"I could still go to the papers."

"You may not like me, but I'd advise you to take
my word about this. You wouldn't want us to have to
leak any of this journal to the papers. It would be a

great embarrassment to you and to your mother and to Margaret. Your brother was a spy and a nasty little pervert. If I were you I'd let the whole thing die away. The biggest favour we can do your family is to keep the journal a secret and destroy it if it ever appears impossible to prosecute him. Now I'd like you to leave my office."

"None of this is really up to you, is it?"

"What do you mean?"

"It's up to the Minister. Or the Cabinet."

"Don't be childish. The High Commissioner will take my advice, and the Minister will take his advice. I'm sure we'd all agree anyway."

"Well, you just do one thing, and I'll leave you alone. You ask the High Commissioner if I can see some of the journal, just enough to prove to me that it exists, that John wrote it, and that he had some kind of reason for what he did, that I can explain."

"Everyone has some kind of reason."

"You just ask the man, and I'll get in touch with you."

Jake went to the door of the office. Allington didn't get up to see him out.

As he walked through the hall toward the elevator, Jake found himself shivering with cold after the long argument. He went down to the main floor, walked out of the building and ran across the road, dodging the traffic instead of finding a safe way to cross. He felt that he couldn't stand still until he'd started to calm down.

As he crossed the square, he was surprised at how many tourists were around, even now in October, feeding the pigeons and taking pictures. The sunlight was warm, but there was a haze in the air that seemed to blend with the grey buildings and the white spray from the fountains.

Jake started to relax and decided to find a restaurant

and eat. He'd phone Margaret and tell her he was going to a movie and wouldn't be home for supper. He went past the National Gallery and started north on Charing Cross Road.

As he made his way along Charing Cross Road, a man came up beside him, turned his head toward him and smiled.

"Mr. Martens," he said. Jake turned.

"I'm a friend of your brother's," the man went on. "Could we go somewhere and talk?"

"Sure," Jake said and then wondered if he meant it. The man beside him was of middle height, balding, and there was something strange about his eyes. He looked and sounded European.

"Perhaps we could go this way," the man said, indicating a street to his right. Jake nodded, and they proceeded down the street and stopped at an Italian restaurant.

"Shall we go in here?"

"I guess so," Jake said. "What do you want to see me about?"

"Come inside please, and we can talk."

"All right."

They went into the restaurant, and Jake watched the man choose a table where they were isolated but had a clear view of the floor and in fact the whole restaurant. Two lines of poetry formed themselves in Jake's mind.

> The world is looking at me.
> I'd better close my eyes.

He took the little red notebook from his pocket and began to write them down.

"What's that?" the man said. He looked a bit tense.

"A notebook," Jake said. "I write poems in it."

"So you're a poet."

"No."

"But you said you write poems."

"I never finish them."

"A great pity. They might be very good."

"I doubt it."

"You will never know if you don't write them."

"If I don't write them I'll know for sure. They can't be good if they're not written."

"Cleverly put."

Jake was annoyed with himself for having got involved in this foolish little contest.

"You said you were a friend of my brother's."

The man looked around the restaurant.

"Yes."

"Do you know where he is?"

The man looked at Jake without answering.

"Were your people at Canada House very helpful?" the man said.

The waiter was coming toward their table, and Jake didn't answer. He wondered why. He had nothing to hide, no secrets. Why did he co-operate in the other man's secrecy in the same way as he co-operated with Allington's anger?

Jake ordered only a cup of coffee, but the man opposite him urged him to eat and himself ordered lasagna.

"Are you sure you won't eat something?" the man said.

"No," Jake said. "I'm not hungry."

The waiter left them, and the man looked back at Jake. As Jake studied his face, he became aware of the strangeness about the eyes; one of the eyes was bigger than the other.

"I saw you leaving Canada House," the man said.

"And you want to know what they told me. What they say about John."

"I'm interested in their reactions, of course." The face that looked at him seemed like a nightmare face, for there might be a threat behind it, not a threat to Jake, but a mysterious unreachable threat to John. What would they do if they knew about the journal? He remembered Allington's remark, and suddenly years of time contracted into this foolish encounter in an Italian restaurant, but Jake couldn't think what it all meant.

In a nightmare when you didn't know what was threatened, you defended yourself or ran.

"They wouldn't tell me anything," Jake said. "They told me to read the newspapers."

"Of course."

The man said nothing more, waiting to see if Jake would continue. It was a sensible thing to do. Jake felt the need to keep talking, to explain.

"What will you tell me?" Jake said. "What do you know?"

"I know that you will do everything you can to help your brother."

"Will I?"

"Of course."

"How do I know what will help him most?"

The waiter came toward them, and again they were silent until he was gone.

"I can assure you that your brother's interests are mine," the man said.

"Does that mean if he goes down you go too?"

"I really do wish to help him, and I know that you do too."

"But that doesn't get us very far. Nothing does until I figure out just what's going on. Canada House has nothing to say, and you have nothing to say."

The man didn't speak.

"Do you know where he is?" Jake said.

The man smiled and took another bite of his lasagna.

"Do you want to help your brother?" the man said as he finished chewing the bite of food. "If he should be

99

in danger, wouldn't you help him?"

"Sure."

"Then you must work with me. That's the only way to help him."

"Maybe."

"Did anyone at Canada House say they wanted to help him?"

Jake smiled at the man and took a drink of his coffee.

"You consider the matter calmly," the man said, "and I think you'll agree with me."

"Maybe," Jake said. He stood up.

"You give the matter some thought," the man said. He took another big bite of the lasagna. A bit of sauce fell on his chin, and he moved it away with his finger.

John turned and walked away, not liking the feeling that he was being watched, studied. He walked out into the street and turned back toward Charing Cross Road, thinking once again that he might go to a movie.

What did they want from him? Some insight into what the people at Canada House and the police knew, perhaps something more long-term. In a way Jake was fascinated by the thought that he was being courted. How quick he'd been to keep silent when the waiter was near; the habit of secrecy came easily to him.

But where was John? Did they know where he was? If they did, would they bother with Jake? Maybe Allington and the police knew where John was. Or was he dead, or had he just gone to earth, vanished in some corner of London to wait? Could he change his appearance and simply disappear? Maybe. Maybe.

11

She sat quietly in the chair where a hundred times she had sat surrounded by the dark city, and as so often, let the music from the radio wrap itself around her until the shapes of sound were more real than those of sight or touch, and she was sitting, not in the room but in the music, thinking of this as some kind of lesson to her of the nature of God and being God's.

Once it seemed to her that she was asleep in her chair, yet she was aware of holding herself from sleep for fear of the nightmares that still returned to shake her as the child died again and again in her arms. This nightmare she could not yet wind in the skein of herself as she must be in God's hands. The nightmare was beyond her grasp, a glimpse of hell perhaps, the one thing that could not, perhaps ever, be made acceptable to her, and so the one thing in her that could not be made acceptable to God, the momentary temptation to say there was no reason, it was only the cruel chance of a moment and then to say what? What question to ask when the only answer had already been put by, and a question could lead only to more questions and to the knowledge that no question could ever be answered except for a moment, this for now, that for now, but laughable or tragic ever to ask for an answer that would continue. Because of that, only the hearts trained to emptiness could be strong.

She opened her eyes and saw the newspaper that still lay beside her where she had dropped it when she saw it made some mention of John. It said nothing, only that there was nothing to be said. The newspapers were devoted to recording what was and what was not that might be, and said that the police were busy going about the business of the law that no-one believed in, because now it was without the guarantee of God's law, that the world was one and that man's actions were seen by the eye of God. That was perhaps the most terrible of all things for a man like John, that he would do right, but that his actions were not seen. He knew no judge who could say yes or no and give him rest, even the pained quiet of knowing himself wrong. What could a man do who had no laws above his laws, no act that tested all his acts, but to be busy in the way he had been taught or to be busy against what he had been taught, but still no more than a slave of consequence, chained to a past that he dragged with him like a heavy shadow.

Her mind went back to the music until it reached an end, and the silence struck her like a blow. Her eyes were open now, and the room was only a room and nothing more, one room that she and John had seen without caring. The child who was the natural eventuality, the pledge that they had, foolishly as might be, faith in the earth, was gone now, and there would not be another. Margaret could no more endure the pain than her body, as it felt its age, could endure the terrifying changes, the new being of the child's conception and growth. She could no longer even endure that her body should be bared or entered, but couldn't tell John why, only knew him as containing himself beside her in the dark or going away from her to be saved from desire.

It had been a long and difficult delivery, and Margaret did not regain consciousness for some time. When she did, she couldn't remember anything of the birth. She lay there with her eyes

102

closed, convinced that the child was dead and that when she opened her eyes they would tell her. So she lay with her eyes closed, though she was conscious and awake. She didn't dare to be told.

She heard voices nearby.

"Yes," she heard the woman's voice say, "isn't he a a fine young chap?"

"We're very pleased," John said.

That gave Margaret the courage to open her eyes and turn her head toward the voices. John and a young nurse were standing by the door. They were both smiling, and Margaret was sure now that it must be all right. The child was alive.

She didn't feel strong enough yet to call out to John, but she lay there with her eyes open, watching him and hoping he would look around and see her. In a few moments he did.

"Margaret," he said as he walked toward her, "how are you feeling?"

She smiled at him.

"I've just seen the baby," he said. "He's a fine baby."

"Can I see him?" She spoke in a whisper.

"I'll ask the nurse." He went out of the room and came back almost immediately.

"She's going to get him now."

Margaret closed her eyes to gather her strength. She opened them as she heard the nurse come in the door. All she could see at first was a bundle of blankets, but the nurse brought the bundle over to her and put it down beside her where she could see the tiny red face. It was asleep, but as it lay there, its face began to change, and it woke and began to cry, a surprisingly small weak cry. Margaret looked at it with a sense of astonishment. This was her child, born from her body. She felt stronger and wanted to hold it against her, but the nurse said to wait, that she would bring the child to be fed a little later on, after Margaret had eaten and rested.

John sat in the chair beside her bed after they had taken the child out. He took her hand and held it for a moment. Margaret smiled at him and then put back her head and

*closed her eyes again. She felt almost faint with the excitement
and happiness of seeing the child. As she lay there, she made
a kind of wordless prayer of happiness and thanksgiving for
the child's birth. She remembered the soaring melody of a
Mozart* Exsultate, Jubilate, *and she wished she could
sing out that joyfulness to God.*

*They brought her food, and the bland hospital diet seemed
to her a particular blessedness, though she wasn't hungry and
ate only a few bites.*

There was magic in the child, an astonishment beyond
speech that the child could be formed inside her and
be in her arms, so small and young. There was something of the magic in all young things. She saw it in
Jacob, the almost man who had come to her to find
something about his brother. There was still something
of a boy's restlessness in him, and it pleased her to
have him in the house, though it gave her pain too, for
her child would not grow to be such a young man,
surprisingly sure and yet innocent, unharmed by all
the things that must be. At first she had been surprised
at his clothes that made him look like a cowboy he
had invented, or some other unexpected man. He was
so thin and pale that his bones seemed to show, and he
was unearthly, like a prophet starving himself to
visions and yet like a boy too who hadn't yet grown
into his body. She wondered if he would invent a life
that was possible or, like so many, blunder down dark
ways until he had beaten out his eyes and could see
nothing, know nothing but pain and hatred and refusal
to be.

Speaking to Jacob about her husband, she felt most
clearly the terror of her ignorance when they had
shared so much. The man who had been her closest
friend had gone a journey she would never go. Her
friendship had given him little, nothing for that journey,
for she herself was far away, bent and hurt, looking for

a word to answer her pain. They had been left no words in common, except for those that told of their shared past. Their memories were the only grip they could have on the thrust of time, the uncontrollable speed of unknown future becoming dead past. But memory was no more than a choice among dead things, a clothing worn to face the unknown, like Jacob's imaginary cowboy, a man who would ride time and call it only a creature wilder than most. Young, he dared to do this, while John had always chosen to deny the impossible rush of time, to believe that each day was the twin of the former and to perfect a pattern of living, to care and know and hold, while she, weak, stupid, only stared at the unfolding revelation and wished to be part of the unfolding, imperfectly always, and always baulking at the moment before the child's death, saying let it not be.

John phoned from the office. He told her that he was being transferred to England as he'd asked. After the child's death he had decided that they ought to move away, for a while at least. Margaret didn't disagree. One place was the same as another.

It was February. A foot of frozen snow lay on the ground, but the roads had been cleared. She stood by the window and saw the new snow begin. She thought about going away. In a way she didn't want to leave, for the child's grave was here. It gave her a solid point at which to begin the daily struggle to accept, to find a new way to live.

Snow began to fall more quickly now, filling the air of the garden and moving with the cold wind. Margaret decided to walk to the cemetery and see the child's grave.

She went upstairs to get a sweater, came down and put on her coat and boots. By the time she stepped out the door, the snow was a blizzard. She took a scarf from her pocket and wrapped it around her head. The wind blew snow into her face. She turned her head down and to one side for shelter

105

as she walked toward the road that led to the cemetery. It was an easy walk in good weather, but in this heavy snow it seemed endless. Margaret was almost pleased with the cold and the snow that hurt her skin. It made the walk to the grave like some kind of pilgrimage.

She knew it would be sensible to go back and make the trip the next day, but she didn't want to be sensible.

The snow began to be slippery underfoot, and she had to walk carefully to keep from losing her balance. The cars that came toward her along the road had their headlights on and were beginning to get covered with snow except for the small patches cleared by the windshield wipers where the drivers peered out, struggling to see through the blizzard. Once or twice cars honked their horns at Margaret to make sure that she saw them in the snow.

All the sounds were muffled. Cars appeared and disappeared almost in silence. The snow grew heavier.

When Margaret reached the hill that led to the cemetery, the road was too slippery, and she had to walk on the snow bank at its side. She climbed the hill with some difficulty, not thinking of anything but reaching the top. When she did finally make it, she was out of breath, and stopped for a moment to rest. She could hear the sound of the snow in the evergreens that were planted on the hill.

She walked into the cemetery. When she looked ahead, she saw only snow and trees and shapes. She knew the way to the grave, even in a blizzard. It was beside the graves of her mother and father. That corner of the cemetery, near the evergreens and just behind a large oak, was so familiar that she could have found it in her sleep. After her mother died, she had come sometimes with her father. When he died, she and John had visited the grave. Now she would only come alone. She could not let John come with her.

She reached the familiar spot and stood in the shelter of the oak tree. She looked at the anonymous earth. There was no headstone for the child. She could not think, yet, of having one.

Margaret walked out of the shelter of the tree and closer to the grave. Again she stood in the strange rushing silence of the blizzard and looked down, as if she could see through the earth to the child. She must get closer to him, her child, her only child.

She lay down on the snow over the grave and pressed her face down into her hands. If only the strength of her desire would melt the snow and the earth. She would reach him, bring him to life. He was there under the earth, like gold, like fire. If only she could reach him.

For a long time she lay there. She didn't feel the cold. She wished the snow would cover her, that she would sleep and die.

That was too easy. She must endure. Her father too lay under the earth here. She couldn't let herself die so easily. She got up and walked away from the grave, cold now and having trouble walking. The blizzard went on around her, and for a moment she thought she was lost, but she found her way to the cemetery gate.

Margaret was empty now. The walk home meant nothing.

When she reached home, John was there.

"Where were you, Margaret?" he said. "I thought you sounded a little upset on the phone so I drove home. I've been awfully worried."

She told him where she had been. He took her snowy clothes from her and brushed them. He put them away and made her a warm drink. She was only annoyed by his attentions to her. She wanted to be left alone.

Getting up from her chair, she walked to the kitchen to prepare a cup of warm milk before going to bed, and before she turned on the light, she stood in the dark room and looked through the window at the branches of the pear tree in silhouette against a light, the shadow that was the Holy Trinity, then switched on the light and began the comforting familiar movements of warming the milk, preparing the cup and sugar, and while the milk was on the stove, going to

107

the bedroom to turn on the electric blanket, all the habitual movements toward sleep which she and John had shared, and now she made alone.

She always got out of bed to nurse the child. There were stories of women falling asleep and letting the baby smother. There was a comfortable chair beside the bed, and as soon as the baby cried, she would get out of bed and sit there. As soon as she heard him and began to get up, the milk would begin to flow. It seemed to her that she hardly slept those nights, for she was often awake and waiting for him before he cried, and after she had fed him, she would lie awake listening to him. He made strange noises as he moved around preparing to sleep. Such little animal noises.

It was lovely and painful to her to hold him at her breast and see the small mouth moving. She could feel the milk going from her body to his.

One night when she had fed him and put him back to bed, she didn't go back to sleep. She was too excited. Quietly so as not to wake John, she went downstairs and put on the record of the Mozart Exsultate, Jubilate that had come to her mind when she first saw the child. She turned the volume very low and sat with her head beside the speaker of the record player, humming quietly with the music. She played it several times. Still she didn't want to sleep. She walked to the window of the living-room and looked out toward the east where, behind the high trees, there was the first sign of light. For a long time she stood there. The sky turned a bright shimmering green as the sun approached, then turned gradually to a pale blue. The sun would rise in a few more minutes. Margaret decided she must go back to bed so she wouldn't be too tired during the day.

John half woke as she got into bed.

"Something wrong?" he said sleepily.

"No," she said, "just go back to sleep."

Listening once again to the music on the radio, she

sat in the soft chair with the strange magical birds on it and drank the warm milk from her cup, slowly, not from hunger or thirst, but as some kind of gesture toward the mysteries of the night and darkness, a preparation, and a deliberate repetition of the act that she and John had shared each night, even when, it seemed now, they shared so little else, and still, sometimes, she set out two cups and then realized that he wasn't here and wondered again where he was and what this could ever mean; she finished her milk and took the cup to wash, wondering now when Jacob would return and making her way to the solitude of her sleep, praying that the nightmare wouldn't come.

The child had his own room and usually slept through the night. When, one morning, they were wakened, not by the child, but by John's alarm, Margaret was surprised that the baby had slept so late. At first she was going to leave him to sleep while she started breakfast, but she decided that she wanted to see him. She walked into the room quietly, just to look at him. The crib was on the other side of the room, and the child's face was away from her. She walked across on tiptoe, a little frightened now as she was every morning by the wonder of her need.

She looked down into the crib, and he looked strange. She couldn't see him breathe. She bent and picked him up, and in that second she knew that he was dead, but would not accept it, held him tightly, silently against her, her eyes closed, holding him tightly, tightly, as if she could bring him back to life.

12

There has been a long break in this. I had a few holidays coming to me and decided that Margaret and I should go away for a trip. We drove to North Wales and found a pleasant farmhouse where we could stay for a few days. The weather was summery, and I spent a lot of time walking. I almost wrote walking and thinking, but there was nothing so conscious as real thought going on, just a kind of relaxed musing.

I had some serious moments, but the fresh air and activity were pleasant, and I came back the stronger for them. I came back resolving not to write any more in this journal. It seemed a weakness. For two weeks and a half I wrote nothing. Tonight I started it again.

Yesterday I met Simon. I thought I had done well, but he wasn't as satisfied as I'd expected. There were several things he'd asked for that I hadn't been able to get. I tried to explain to him. He's a professional. He devotes his life to taking risks, but I can't behave like that. I wish he'd try to understand my position. I want to get him the material he needs, but it isn't always possible.

I have a couple of things planned. I've arranged a meeting with the Defence people at Grosvenor Square. The British have a tentative training plan that doesn't need action yet but will provide an excuse for me to ask questions. Simon wants to know about what we have in the north and about the amount of building that's going on there.

Jim Allington seems to be around my office a lot lately. He always seems to be on the point of saying something, but doesn't say it. I get the impression that he really wants to make friends, but doesn't quite know how to go about it. I wonder what he wants from me? To climb up, using me as a stepping-stone. Perhaps not. He may be human. I feel the need of talking to someone certainly, but not to him.

Once or twice recently, I've tried to talk to Margaret, but it's hard to find anything we have in common anymore. I talk about the office, but my real problem there, how to get material I don't have, that perhaps no-one there has, is something that I can't explain. We talk a little about people we've met, those we know, but there is little to say about them. I asked Margaret tonight if she wanted to go to a play sometime, but she wasn't very interested. I think I'll get tickets for something that I think she'd like.

I watched her again tonight through the bathroom keyhole as she undressed to get her bath. She was always shy about undressing in front of me, and since the child's death more than shy. Even before sometimes I'd quietly creep up to the bathroom door and watch her. She is very white, with low, heavy hips.

What would happen if she knew I was watching her? She would simply retreat farther into herself, into a deeper silence.

He had become very happy now. His files were growing so rapidly that he couldn't help being happy. And then, last night, the pile of letters in the bedroom, hidden away at the back of the drawer and tied with a piece of rough twine. There were thirty-four letters in the bundle, the handwriting obviously a woman's, but they were signed only with the initial G. He had set up a new file for them, cross-referenced to the owner and also to the letter G in case something should turn up. Once or twice that

111

kind of cross reference had turned up trumps for him, revealing a sudden important piece of information. The man himself appeared to be of no importance, but it was hard to be sure. What he must do for now was to collect and file his documents, to contain all his secrets. Imagine knowing all the secrets in the world. From whom no secrets are hid. He went back to his files, happy, very happy, and began to cross reference and collate, to make lists of wanted documents.

Time passes. I always get a shock when I look back at a previous passage of this and see that everything is different, yet the same, same problems, same worries. Day by day time passes, and I can't lay my hands on it or anything. What have I done that I can see, that I can hold in my hands? Sometimes I wish terribly that the child had lived, that some part of me could go on. Stupid egotism that afflicts me when I'm tired. No part of me matters, only what I can do, what I can give. I suppose if the child had lived, the difference would have been that some part of me did matter, at least temporarily, that the effort given to the child was real and personal, the self-abnegation for something closer at hand.

I took Margaret to a play, Shakespeare's *Richard II*. Why was it that all through the play I kept thinking of Simon? Perhaps because he seems to live on the level of political realities as large as those facing a mediaeval king. I found myself likening this journal to Richard's vague speculations when he should have been acting. But I am not a king; my field of action is so limited that I might as well speculate. *Speculum* meant mirror, didn't it? At least in the Renaissance. To speculate is to look in a mirror? What about scientific speculation? Just a change in the meaning of the word, I suppose.

Today I had a meeting at Grosvenor Square and got some of the information that Simon has been asking for. Not all of it, and he'll no doubt demand the rest, but still I was pleased at being able to get what I did, since it wasn't directly related to what I was there for.

The whole struggle is a struggle for the control of time. We see it as a battle for places or for men or for power, but finally it is simply a battle for the power of directing time. To control a place is only important if you continue to control it. No-one can control it forever; no-one and no group can do this except that by causing a break in time, a separation of the future from the past, all time is changed.

The present is the only present we're ever given.

I met Simon again to discuss the information I've just got. He's still not satisfied. He doesn't say so, but I can tell. He's so distant. The praise he sometimes offers me is entirely superficial. I can tell he doesn't mean it, that he's bored with me, an unimportant agent, and simply goes through the motions of asking for information, praising me for what I get, insisting on more. I wondered today if he's in trouble with his superiors, if they're dissatisfied with what he's getting from me or with what he's able to get from his other agents. He has others, I'm sure, and some that are more important than I am. I don't know why I know that, just something about his attitude, always a bit preoccupied. Perhaps it's deliberate.

He read over the series of notes once more, pleased that they seemed to hold together, to tell just enough. It was dangerous to seem to know too much. They wouldn't believe it and would demand some kind of documentary proof. And all he could offer them was the scraps of paper on which he made his notes, on which he invented the secrets that he gave them.

He wondered if they would ever catch on. Eventually they must, but he'd tried not to be stupid about it, and it might take them a while. But what would they do if they found out? Would they think that he was working for the other side?

It wasn't that at all. He invented things to tell them for the sheer pleasure of it, for the pleasure of having things to tell.

Simon told me today not to hurry too much in getting what he wants, but to make long-term plans if it was necessary. I said he was treating me like a fool. He didn't react much to my anger. He lives so far behind his eyes that I'm never sure that any emotion reaches him.

I've had to attend three receptions this week and really haven't felt up to it. I must relax. When I see Simon again, I'll tell him he's pushing me too hard. I suppose that's why he told me to take my time. Our next meeting is some time off.

I haven't written anything for several days. I find that late in the evenings I'm bored and think of getting this out, but I don't want to think about anything so I just go to bed. I've bought a handful of mysteries to read for relaxation. They don't help much. Perhaps long Victorian novels. What nonsense. I must put this away.

Nothing to write. Should I describe the weather?

I've gradually been accumulating a bit of material. I'm to meet Simon in ten days.

Two days of frantic sexual excitement. It seems to be letting up now. I found myself staring at every woman I met. There was one moment. Why go on?

Waiting.

Allington's Folly: Everything he does.

I've been reading *Barchester Towers*. Not a bad distraction, but a bit silly. I've tried to do some serious reading and thinking and find that it's very difficult. I can't even be bothered to finish the long and boring analyses of the latest economic crisis in the papers. What can they say that they haven't said several times before?

I've had a request from Ottawa to initiate discussions about some new problems related to the training plan. This will give me a week or so of concentrated work and may also turn up something for Simon. Some of it is material I've gone over before, but there are some new things that will involve more Defence people.

I've finished the work on the training plan. I decided that I wouldn't take out this journal until I'd got all that out of the way. I've got a bit out of the habit of keeping the journal lately. I'll be meeting Simon again in two days. I've used three films since our last meeting. I hope this time he's satisfied. I really have done my best for him. He ought to realize that.

I was very foolish today. I met Simon, and I found again that while he said he was pleased with what I'd got him, he didn't seem to take it very seriously. It was good material, both important and very secret. I made a speech about the danger I was running and how I was doing the best I could for him. He just looked at me from somewhere far back in that cold head of his and watched me make a fool of myself. I have the feeling that he'll trust me less from now on. There was no point in saying what I did. I know that, but I couldn't help but try to make him realize what I was doing, that it mattered to me to do something in the world, something for the future, and that his refusal to take me seriously was undermining me.

I knew that I couldn't expect him to care, that he was merely a professional doing his job as coolly and perfectly as he could.

After my outburst he offered me money and that made me even angrier, but I controlled myself and didn't say any more. I just refused the money as curtly as I could and tried to conclude our business, but he decided to talk. Everything he said was obvious, that we must proceed one step at a time, that I had my job and he had his, and that we were both adding our small bit to the improvement of things, but it did calm me to hear him say these things, even though I'd said them to myself a hundred times already. Still, he was holding back a great deal of himself. I suppose that's his job.

He has several new requests this time, and fortunately they seem to be things that I can lay my hands on.

Later this afternoon, Jim Allington came to see me and asked if something was bothering me. He said I'd seemed tense lately and "he and the High Commissioner" had wondered if there was anything they could help with. He really is a disgusting snoop.

I tried to make a joke of the whole thing. I said it was just old age and hypochondria creeping up on me. It seemed foolish to hide the fact that I'd been tense, but I tried to simply admit it and explain away the possibility that there was any serious reason. Said I'd had a couple of dodgy jobs to do and that Margaret hadn't been well. I said that if I felt the need to be relieved of my duties, I'd let the High Commissioner know about it. That was a good stroke and left him without too much to say. It is after all the High Commissioner's business, not his.

Tonight I decided to reread this journal. I was amazed at how much I've written over these last months.

Seeing everything foreshortened and crowded together in the journal, there seemed no justification for my tension and nervousness. My confidence two or three months ago seems so simple, so close to me, that the loss of it makes no sense. Yet the time has gone by, slowly, painfully, day by day, and I have lost that sense of confidence and sureness. I still feel that what I have done is right, that it was necessary for me to act, to become a new man, but when I face the morning and ask what I am to do today, what actions will mean something to me, I find it hard to step forward with much confidence.

I suppose I must once more concentrate on the future, on the meaning of my commitment, the new man that I have become, and try to regain the sense of possibility. It's so easy for the meaning to be lost in the detail. I suppose I said that earlier on, in a different context. One of the aphorisms. I've made few recently. One sign of the tension, that aphorisms no longer come to me as they used to.

Commitment should not depend on hope. It's a weak and silly thing that depends on hope. Funny how that slips by in the famous bit from Corinthians. Faith, hope and charity. Faith, yes, and charity, no doubt. But isn't hope a watered-down version of faith? Hope is faithless faith.

Perhaps I'm recovering. I made an aphorism.

What do I hope for? Nothing. But I have some kind of faith. I'm pointed toward a future that will be better than the present. What soft words those are. It's hard to find words that are hard enough and yet look forward.

I thought this afternoon as I left the office that there was someone following me. I went into a newsagent's and got an *Evening News* and then went back into the office. It seems unlikely that anyone would be following me, but I returned to the office as quickly as I could.

APHORISMS

My first act of commitment to the future was to will the continuation of my past.
The immediate purpose of a man's actions blinds him to their real meaning.
The Monroe doctrine is nothing but an old and repeated threat, no better for the age and repetition.
The job of a civil servant is to be paid for doing things he believes wrong.
The future is perfect because it does not exist.
One can't be at ease with all one's allies.
Freedom is being at one with history.
The present is the only present we're ever given.
Allington's Folly: everything he does.
Hope is faithless faith.

I've always had a weakness for aphorisms. I remember in university, I used to collect them. Pascal was a gold mine.

Le silence éternel de ces espaces infinis m'effraie.

That seems to be the only one that's stuck in my mind. I'm sure I used to know some of Oscar Wilde's. Why do I remember them now only half right, when they depend entirely on the perfection of wording?

An aphorism says everything and means nothing.

It's hard to sustain excitement in the face of petty failures.

13

When Jake woke in the morning, he felt as if he'd hardly been asleep. The interview with Allington and the other with the man in the restaurant seemed to have gone on all night, but confused in the dream so that Jake was being accused and tempted by Allington and John, while the man with the strange eyes just sat and ate and watched. Jake wished he could talk to Member or someone about it all, try to clear his mind of it.

He heard the noise of dishes rattling. Margaret must be up. Jake threw back the covers and climbed out of bed, the air of the room sharp against his bare skin but not cold enough to be unpleasant. He pulled on his clothes, washed himself and walked down the hall toward the kitchen.

"Hi," he said as he walked in.

"How did you muh ... muh ... make out yesterday?" she said.

"I'm not sure. Allington and I didn't get along too well. We spent most of the time arguing. But I suppose he told me most of what there is to tell. He's going to ask the High Commissioner whether I can see parts of the journal John kept."

Before the last word was finished, Jake regretted what he'd said. There were a dozen reasons why he should have kept his mouth shut. Margaret didn't speak, only nodded her head. She lifted the tray of food in front of her.

119

"Come into the dining-room and we'll have some breakfast."

The room they entered had a strange quality that revealed, in a way that Jake couldn't explain, that it had never been meant as a dining-room but was a makeshift created when the house had been broken up into apartments.

They ate almost in silence. Jake felt awkward, aware that he had stayed two days now without making any plans about leaving. He'd soon have to decide what he was going to do, but at the moment his feelings were suspended somewhere. He could only wait and see.

Part of the confusion was the strange situation with John. Jake had assumed that when he came to England, he would find out the truth, or at least certain key facts to tell his mother and that, once these were found, he'd know the job was over. But as things had worked out, he'd learned very little. Only about the existence of the journal, really, and the hints that Allington had given him about its contents. That and the fact that the others were interested.

John had thrown over everything that made up his life, all the things that had been important to him. If only Jake could see some of the journal, he felt that he might sense what it meant. The existence of the journal fascinated him. Writing it was such a foolish thing to do. To write a journal must mean that he wanted someone to read it, to understand, but not Allington, not the police. How much understanding would he find there?

Jake looked at Margaret as she sat opposite him eating a piece of toast and jam, and he remembered what Allington had said about his brother being a nasty little pervert. Jake found himself looking away from Margaret as he thought of that. He was inclined to doubt everything Allington said, but he wanted desperately to see the journal, to try and understand the man he'd hardly known who was his brother. It would be almost like being able to talk to him.

They looked so little alike that no-one would have taken them for brothers, especially with the sixteen years' difference in their ages. Jake found himself wondering for a moment if one or the other could be illegitimate, but it was unthinkable that a woman as simple and devoted as his mother could have deceived her husband. It must simply be that John resembled his mother's family and Jake his father's. His mother had once said something, not directly but just something in passing, that suggested to Jake that she thought he was like his father. Jake had wondered at the time what she meant. He could remember nothing about his father. When he was younger, he'd sometimes go into the room that had been his father's study, where the books still sat in neat rows on the small bookshelf. A brown chair, brown books, a serious room. Jake had always imagined his father as a man of great personal intensity. Sometimes when he stood in the room, very silently and with his eyes closed, he would imagine that the old man was still there, looking at him, perhaps displeased. A solitary man, Jake was convinced he had been that.

There was the man in the restaurant to think about too. Probably Jake should tell the police, but he knew he wouldn't. He'd made a bond of secrecy with the man, without ever really intending to. Jake wondered what he'd do if the man approached him again.

Jake finished his breakfast and had a second cup of coffee. He stood up.

"That was good," he said. "Thanks a lot."

She smiled and nodded.

"I don't know when I'll be back," he said. "I might be pretty late, but I can let myself in."

"Fine," she said.

Jake walked out of the room. He'd decided to walk

121

to Hattersley's place, but he had time to spare. He looked forward to helping the squatters. So far as he knew, the housing supply in Canada had never been so bad that people turned to squatting, but it might get that way in the big cities. Squatting was a whole new kind of revolutionary act for him, a different kind of civil disobedience aimed directly at property.

Jake postponed once again the decision about how soon to give up asking questions about John and go back to face his mother. Tomorrow, he thought, he'd have another try at seeing the journal, maybe go to the hostel where John had stayed and see what turned up.

He walked on toward Hattersley's place, first walking west along Cromwell Road and then north through Kensington. It took him less than an hour, and he knocked on the door of the basement room just before ten-thirty. The girl with the dark hair opened the door.

"Hi," she said. "Don's gone out, but he'll be back in a few minutes. Come on in."

She was wearing a short dress, and Jake noticed how attractive she was, even though her clothes were worn and crumpled, as if she had slept in them. The day before she'd spent most of her time sitting on the bed in a dark corner of the room, and he hadn't noticed her much.

"You want some coffee?" she said.

"If you're making it."

"What else is there for me to do?"

Jake looked at her. There was no expression on her face that seemed to go with the remark.

"Did you come over here with Don?"

"I came first, but we arranged to meet here."

"How do you like it?"

"I don't."

"Why not?"

"Just look at this place. I sit around here all day

long and try to convince myself that I don't really wish I was home and living someplace decent. I can't get a job cause I've already overstayed my visa, and if they catch me they might send me back. Not that I'd really mind."

"Couldn't you get a better place?"

"Revolutionaries don't live in nice places. They live among the people. The common people can't wait to get out of here, but the revolutionaries never want to get out and live someplace that's clean and warm.

"You're bitter."

"You know what I'd like? I'd like to be riding in a big vulgar American car down a big vulgar American road to Macdonalds to have two nineteen-cent hamburgs and two orders of French fries and two chocolate milk shakes."

"Why'd you come over then?"

"God, I've thought about that a lot recently, and I think it was just the whole sex thing. He was the first guy that really turned me on, and it was too much. I got it all confused with politics and love and everything else. When he was coming over here to school, I just couldn't stand it, to be separated from him. I never thought that there could be lots of guys, that all the excitement was in me, not in him. Anyway, when he came over, I came too. Then he quit school and moved here, and I started to think I wasn't really a revolutionary." She stopped for a minute.

"I'm really giving you the works, aren't I?" she said. "But you're the first person I've met for months who wasn't either English or so busy talking about revolution that I wouldn't dare open my mouth. And I can't talk to the English ones, they seem like foreigners."

"Why?"

"I don't know. They're just different from us."

They heard a noise at the front door, and the girl

gave Jake his cup of coffee and put the kettle back on the gas ring.

Hattersley walked into the room. He said hello to Jake and kissed the girl on the back of the head. She didn't say anything, but went and sat down on the bed.

"Are you ready to go?" Hattersley said.

Jake nodded.

"Did they tell you anything about your brother?"

"Not much. I'm still working on it." He didn't mention the other. He wouldn't.

"You won't get far."

"I don't want to make it too easy for them."

Jake felt how hard it was to keep from looking over at Lucy on the sofa. He wanted to see the expression on her face, to guess what she was thinking.

Tom Walsh stuck his head around the door.

"Are you coming then?"

Hattersley jumped up.

"On our way. See you later, Loo," he said to the girl as they walked out. She didn't answer.

The three men crowded into the front of the enclosed van.

"Jack's over there already," Tom said. "He's helping her pack up her bits of stuff."

"Did you drive past the house today?" Hattersley said.

"It looks fine. A few broken windows, but we can soon set that straight."

"Whose house is it?" Jake said.

"The council's going to tear it down. Widening the road, but they won't do it for months."

They pulled up beside a big old house. Along the side were piles of rubbish, a broken bicycle frame and a couple of car seats with half the stuffing pulled out.

Tom led the way into the front hall, where he knocked on the first door. The house smelled of urine, and the walls were damaged and stained.

"Come in," someone shouted.

The room seemed to be full of children. A pair of them, half-dressed, were fighting over an old doll while an older brother demanded that they stop and put it in a box he was holding. A baby was asleep in a baby carriage in the corner of the room. There was a hole in the ceiling above him and beside it the plaster had fallen from the walls.

A woman, something less than thirty, with her coat on and wild hair of a nondescript brown looking as if she hadn't had time to brush it for weeks, walked over to the children and slapped each of the two who were fighting on the leg, took the doll and put it in the box. The two children began to cry and blame each other, incoherently, and with words that they still couldn't perfectly form.

The floor of the small room was full of suitcases and boxes, and in a corner a young man with a beard and a grey turtleneck sweater was emptying drawers into another large box.

"I don't know where I'm at," the woman said, "and you've got the van here already. Oh do shut up, Susie and Lise, and let me get on with it." She looked frantically toward the three men who'd just walked into the room.

"You could take the pram out," she said, "and we'd have a bit more room here."

Jake and Tom Walsh moved toward the sleeping baby.

"Be careful you don't wake him," she said.

They carried the baby outside. He stirred, but didn't wake. They went back in.

The two girls were dressed now, and their mother pushed them toward the door.

"You play outside, and when we're ready to go I'll buy you a sweetie."

"I want it now," the older one said, and they both

125

stopped and looked back. The mother reached in the pocket of her coat and brought out two pennies.

"Go along to the shop and get your sweetie then."

The two of them took the pennies and raced out chattering to each other.

"Oh where was I?" the mother said.

"Slow down," Tom said, "you'll do yourself a damage getting into a state like that."

"Jake and I will start carrying," Hattersley said, "while you people finish getting the rest of it packed." He led the way to the front window where they picked up a mattress that lay on the floor. They took it out to the truck and came back for more. It was hard to climb over the boxes and suitcases, but they gradually got things moved out. There wasn't a lot.

"Do they all live in that room?" Jake said after they'd put a couple more mattresses in the back of the truck.

"That's it," Hattersley said. "One room for the six of them and share the lav with the rest of the house. When it's working."

"Does she have a husband?"

"He's at work, I imagine. They weren't too badly off till he got sick last year. He's been back at work for a month now."

The two little girls came back from the store and tried to get in the house, but their mother pushed them back outside. They took up a position on the pavement and watched the van being packed.

Once when Jake came back out of the house with a box, he found that they had climbed in the back and were looking in the boxes for some favourite toy.

"Out you come," he said and took them, one at a time, under the arms and swung them up into the air and away to the sidewalk.

"Do that again," the smaller one said, and Jake lifted her up and swung her in the air.

126

"Now me," the other said, and Jake swung her too, high in the air while she laughed and screamed.

"All right now," Jake said, "I've got to get back." He walked into the house and picked up another box from the room that was almost bare. As he walked out of the house and looked at the two children standing there in their oddly assorted clothes, he wondered how many years it had been since he'd touched a small child.

"Do you want to go again," he said, putting out his hands to them.

They both ran toward him. He picked up the first one and swung her in the air over his head, back and forth and around.

"You can fly," he said, "Look how you can fly." She spread her arms like wings, then screamed and grabbed his wrists again. He put her down and picked up the other.

"You're a bird," Jake said, "floating through the air." He whirled her round, but his arms got tired.

"Again, again," they cried.

"Have to work" Jake said. He went back in the house. Hattersley was sitting on the floor. The others had stopped work for a minute and were scattered around the room sitting on boxes or chairs.

"Are you all quitting?" Jake said.

"Tea break," Tom Walsh said. "But we've lost the tea pot."

"Hey," Hattersley said from the floor, "you haven't met these people, have you?"

"Just Tom."

"That's Tom's brother Jack, and this is Doreen. Jake's a Canadian. His brother's the spy who's in all the papers."

"Really?" Doreen said.

Jake nodded.

"That's a funny thing, isn't it?" she said. "What do you think about him?"

"I don't know. I can't really find out much about it. I guess he thought it was the right thing."

"But selling out your country," she said. "I don't know about that."

"Your country hasn't done a hell of a lot for you," Hattersley said.

"Still and all," she said, "it's not natural, is it?"

"Come on, you lot," Tom said. "A little less theory and a little more action. We've still got loads of work."

They all started to work again. Jake wondered why it was he wanted to defend John. He picked up a box and carried it outside. The children were waiting for him, wanting to be swung again. He picked them up and swung them, a little less heartily this time.

Within another few minutes they had everything packed, and then they realized that they had to put four adults and three children in the van too. They all laughed and got a bit hysterical as they tried different methods of fitting everyone in, but they did succeed, and Jake found himself huddled in a corner with a child on his knees. The little girl was giddy from all the excitement and kept trying to pinch his nose. Jake turned his face away and tried to think of some way to distract her, but she was persistent, and he began to get impatient. He kept calling her attention to things that were sticking out of the boxes around them and asking her what they were, and he succeeded in this way in keeping her fairly still until they stopped and Tom shouted "Everybody out."

They opened the doors and tumbled out. In front of them was a small brick house. Some of the windows were boarded up. It was the corner house of a long row of terrace houses, and the narrow road beside it turned sharply and ran under the new motorway. Even now, when the traffic was light and the motorway not in use, the cars were having to slow down to pass the corner.

As they stood on the pavement sorting themselves out after the crowded ride, Jack Walsh went round the side of the house and over the brick wall. A couple of minutes later he came out the front door.

"Are you coming in?" he said, "or are you going to stay out there all day?"

They each grabbed a suitcase or a box and made their way to the front door. The house had a damp, unused smell, but it seemed to be in livable condition.

Doreen and the children began exploring the upstairs, the children laying claim to various rooms, Doreen carrying the baby, who was now hungry and crying. When she came back downstairs, she stood jiggling the baby to quiet it and looked at Tom.

"It's grand, isn't it? Do you think they'll let us stay?"

"Don't know, but we'll fight for it. They might give you tenancy for a few months till they're ready to tear it down. Let's bring in your bits from the van and lock the door before anyone gets here."

The four young men went out and began to unload. They brought everything into the front room and dumped it there, so that it didn't take long to get the van empty. Then Tom took it back to the place he'd borrowed it, and the rest went inside the house.

They barricaded the doors and then began to sort out the things they'd put down in the front room. It was well on in the afternoon by the time they were finished. Jack lit a fire in the fireplace and Doreen made them a cup of tea. Not long after that Tom came back with some beer. He said that a few people on the street seemed to be coming by for a look, but there were no signs of anyone else.

After drinking a bottle of beer on an empty stomach, Jake felt quietly and happily distant from the noise of the house as Doreen tried to settle the children. He was elated at having a part in her obvious happiness, at seeing this empty house filled with the noise and movement of people who needed it.

He thought of how recently he had been in Canada arguing with Member. He thought of John, the Italian restaurant, Margaret making her solitary meal somewhere a few miles away. So strange. That these things were all around him.

Someone knocked at the door. Tom looked out the window.

"It's Billy," he said, and went to open the door. Jake could hear him moving the things in front of the door.

"How are you, Billy Duffin?" he said when he'd let the man in.

"Not too bad, Tom, not too bad."

"What do you think of the new place?"

"It's all right isn't it?"

He walked into the room. He was a short small man with something about his sharp features that looked like those of a man who'd been sick and would be sick again soon. Jake thought it was something in the eyes. He wore a navy duffel coat and looked a bit awkward as he walked into the front room where they were all sitting.

"I'll go round and get something for tea," Doreen said.

"Listen," Tom said, "if you're going to be feeding all this lot, you'd better take this." He pulled out a ten-shilling note.

"No, Tom," she said. "The least we can do is give you some tea."

Tom put away the note and went to let Doreen out. When he came back, he offered one of the bottles of beer to Billy who took it and sat down. There was still a kind of awkwardness, but within a few minutes he and Tom began to joke a little, and by the time Doreen had got back with the food, they'd all relaxed again.

130

Doreen put some sausages and baked beans in pans on the fireplace, and the smell of them as they cooked made Jake feel even hungrier than he was already. When she handed him a plate of food, he ate it in what seemed like half a dozen bites and could have eaten more. While they were drinking their tea, Doreen started to put the two girls to bed.

As it began to get dark outside, the room got very dim. They'd run out of fuel, and the fire started to die away.

"Well," Tom said, "it looks as if you're set for one night."

"Do you think they'll come in the morning?" Doreen said.

"I don't know. One or two of us will stay the night to see that you're all right."

"There's no need for that, Tom," Billy said.

"If you don't want us then."

"I didn't say that."

"I'll sleep as well here as at home. Save me moving. But I'll go if you like."

"I don't want you to put yourself out any more than you have."

"I wouldn't mind staying either," Hattersley said. "I'd be wondering how things were anyway."

"Suit yourselves," Billy said.

"I think I might as well take off now," Jake said and stood up.

"Could you stop off on your way," Hattersley said, "and tell Loo that I'm going to stay the night here?"

"If you like," Jake said.

"Do you know the way?"

"Not really."

Hattersley gave Jake directions and Tom let him out and then barricaded the door behind him. As Jake walked away from the house he felt suddenly lonely, leaving behind the man and woman in their home, the children he had swung into the air. He walked on and remembered what Lucy had said to him that morning. He wondered how she'd react to the message he was bringing. That morning, when she'd opened the door for him, he'd been so surprised at how pretty she was and then surprised again at the things she'd told him.

When he reached Hattersley's place, he walked in the outside door and knocked on the door of the basement room. It seemed to take a long time for her to come.

"It's you," she said.

Jake nodded, and she moved aside to let him walk in.

"Don sent me with a message. He's staying overnight to make sure they're all right."

"Should I care?" she said.

Jake didn't say anything, just shrugged his shoulders. He closed the door, and she turned and looked at him. She was only a few feet away from him as they stood, looking steadily at each other. Jake could see the shape of her breasts under the dress, the almost heavy bare thighs.

"I want to stay here tonight," he said. "Do you want me to?"

She nodded a little.

14

Why should anyone be following me? I've reconsidered each meeting with Simon, each time I've had files home, and I can't think of a time when I could have been discovered, unless they already know about him. Could that be it?

Could Simon's people be following me? That makes no sense. He knows what I'm doing. But if the British know about me, they must know about him. So why follow me? Why not just arrest me now? There's nothing I can lead them to.

I'm still not sure that I'm being followed, but once or twice I've thought so.

What will I do when I'm to meet Simon next week? Just be very careful.

Why is it that all personal tensions come out in me as sexual excitement? When I'm relaxed and happy there's none of the febrile eroticism that has possessed me recently. I have no idea why this should be so. It seems to be almost a physical thing, that certain kinds of nervous excitement set all my nerves on edge with the result being this strange nervous frustration. There's something unhealthy about it.

I suppose there's no point in speculating about it. There's nothing I can do.

I suppose I must tell Simon that I think I've been followed. I hate to. Already it seems to me that he doesn't think much of my performance. This will only make me seem more dangerous and less useful for him. Still, whatever he thinks about it, I've done what I've done, and I wouldn't alter it. To have done more was not possible. To have done less would have made me a lesser man. I will continue and do what I can. There is a new world coming, and I have life only to the extent that I am part of that world.

Confusion is the normal state when anything important happens. I remember what little my father would tell me about the Russian revolution. He said nobody had any clear idea what was happening. It all seemed to be random activity, troop movements, deaths, fighting,

133

demonstrations. In some places nothing seemed to happen at all. Sometimes many months passed before a district commissar would arrive and tell people that there had been a revolution, that their whole world had changed. People only have a sense of what life was like before such an event and what life was like after the event, with little or no sense of what the event itself was, how it came about or whether it happened easily or with great difficulty and bloodshed. How can we ask the meaning of any small act?

Intellectuals sit on the bank looking for patterns on the bottom of the river while everyone else is crossing. The intellectual never drowns, but never crosses.

I went to a movie tonight. Asked Margaret if she wanted to go, and for a moment, I thought she would say yes, but she finally said no. I wonder if she is starting to come out of her isolation and feel part of the world again. What would I feel if that happened? Have I left her behind entirely? After years of living together, I think I could still maintain a life with her even though I have another life that must matter more.

I found myself strangely involved with the movie. It was not very good, but my emotions were very quick to respond even to somewhat artificial situations.

That day in the Midlands. Her picture, almost un-recognizable in *Time*. The threat, the feeling of the omen. Ominous.

He sat in the station waiting-room which was only a little less cold than the platform outside. How was it he had seen it here? How did events choose their settings?

It was on the train that he looked at the magazine, and when he realized what it meant, his head began to spin, and he thought he might faint.

Imagined her body broken. Her body that was what? A waiting-room. A dead drop where one left messages, not knowing if they were received. Or by whom.

A dead drop. And came out living.

I wonder how my mother is? She's geting old, nearly seventy now. Perhaps I ought to phone her one day soon. It's been two years now since I've seen her, and Margaret has been less regular in her correspondence than she used to be. I suppose she still has Jacob close by. I wonder if he goes home often? This afternoon I suddenly thought how fine it would be to be home in her kitchen and eating fresh bread that she'd baked, or rolls with poppy seeds on them and drinking a cup of hot coffee, perhaps talking about old friends. Does she still keep a garden?

I suppose what I'm thinking about is innocence, and I'm too old to have that. Or is it age? Is this a world in which it's no longer possible to be innocent? Because we know too much. And it's not possible to know less except by deliberately shutting out information, and that isn't an innocent act. All the romantic attempts to return to the past are like that, refusals, deliberate acts of blindness.

What does my mother think of the world? Of Jacob or of me? In her case there are things she will never know, but not because of any wilful ignorance. There are things that are like notes she can't hear or a language that she's never learned. I suppose that's it, a kind of language that she's never learned. A language that I can follow and perhaps speak, haltingly and self-consciously. It is partly a sense of closeness. The nearness of destruction, the foreshortening of all perspectives.

Perspective. An invention of the Renaissance, which also invented history, perhaps invented time. There are no longer any vistas.

I'll phone my mother now. It's about supper-time in Canada.

Yesterday when I phoned my mother, she couldn't believe at first that I was calling from England. The long-distance call made her nervous, and she found it hard to talk. I chattered pointlessly about Margaret and the weather and my work. It didn't matter what I said so long as I made clear that I had called to wish her well. I asked about Jacob and she said he's well. We didn't talk for long, but I think the call pleased her. After I'd hung up, I suddenly found myself feeling very lonely. There was a knowledge of how far I've come since my youth and the impossibility of going back or even really understanding what I was then.

How did it all start? With Margaret. If I hadn't met her, I'd perhaps have become a small-town high-school teacher, something of that sort. I wouldn't have thought of entering External (and wouldn't have got in) if it hadn't been for her father. It's strange to think of a man so rigorously and obviously upright using his influence to help me get into the department. It never seemed to him that there could be anything wrong with it, I suppose. He'd met me and considered me a decent potential husband for his daughter and a decent potential member of External, and that was sufficient evidence. I must have done well on the exam, but I never doubted that it was his influence that got me in. I'm not a born member of the governing classes, although it's hard to say what class I was born to be a member of. From what I can gather, my father had a few connections in the lower aristocracy, but my mother seems to be a woman of almost peasant background. And then what does European background mean in Canada?

Why am I so concerned with the past these days?

As an escape, I suppose, from the confusions that surround me. As I left the office this afternoon, I thought again that I was being followed. I decided to cross over to the National Gallery and do a bit of testing, walking in and out of rooms and doubling back. I'm still not sure whether or not I was being followed. I've found an odd roundabout route which, used properly, should ensure that no-one can follow me.

I wonder what Simon will say when I tell him I think I'm being followed. Perhaps he'll know already. That's not impossible. But if he does, if he's responsible, it will be a pleasure to explain how I've lost them.

The complexities of a big city lend themselves to ingenious manipulation.

What will happen if my plan fails?

Today as I walked through the Gallery, everyone I saw seemed to have a familiar face and seemed to be watching me more than the paintings. When I'm nervous I often get the feeling that I'm being watched. Could that be the reason that I think I'm being followed? I suppose it's common for people who are a bit shy to feel that they're being watched. Could I really call myself shy any longer? There was a time when I was, the early days in Ottawa, when I was just beginning to find my way and astonished at being close to power or what seemed like power in those placid days.

Think of the words that encode the time since then. Suez. Cuba. Hungary. Kennedy. Krushchev. Sinai. Oswald. Vietnam. Enough there to define a new world. And that is the language my mother doesn't understand? She could explain those words, some of them anyway, but they don't immediately create for her the meaning of the present. I suspect my brother speaks this language. But then what does Suez mean to him? Perhaps I include it only because I've been in England for two years, and here it's the fall from grace, the expulsion from the Garden.

Why do I feel so close to the end of something? It's almost as if I were preparing to move away. The poetry of departures. Perhaps I've completed some stage in my own development.

When I tell Simon I'm being followed, I suppose we'll have to make some new arrangement, just use the mailing address or something of that sort. I can leave that to him. It's his business and he'll know what's best.

I'm tired, but too excited to go to bed yet. After tomorrow things will be so much clearer.

Why do I sit here in the middle of the night writing letters to myself? I can't help it. I need to talk to someone, need someone to share what I'm doing, but Simon is no real help and there's no-one else. That would be the greatest gift, the chance to talk to someone, to explain and find out their opinion, to have company in what I'm doing would be a great relief and help to me.

It grows later and later, but I cannot make myself go to bed. The flat and the street outside are so quiet at this time of night that it seems that something must be wrong.

Met Simon this afternoon.

When I met him that day and told him, he tried not to react, but I could tell that he was upset. He asked me to describe the man I'd seen and I told him that I couldn't be sure, that at different times it had seemed to be different people. I told him that I'd wondered sometimes if it might be my imagination. I shouldn't have said that. He seemed to lose interest then, as if anyone weak enough to have imagined such a thing could be of no use to him.

He asked if they'd followed me that day. I told him how I'd come, where I'd changed trains carefully three times.

After a few minutes he cut off the meeting, without giving me any new request for material. I asked him what he wanted next. He said he thought we should let it rest for now. I asked how long. He said we'd have to wait and see. He said that if everything looked safe, he'd be in touch with me. It was one of those remarks that meant some vague sometime in a possible future and that I was not to ask questions.

Here I am, useless. After he left, I found myself wandering pointlessly around strange streets until I felt hungry. I went into a little restaurant and ordered a meal, but when I got it, I couldn't eat, and I paid and left. The woman was very upset that I hadn't eaten my meal and followed me to the door asking if I was sure I was all right.

Once as I walked down the street, I thought I saw Simon on a bus that went past me. If it had stopped nearby, I think I would have run after it, silly as that would be.

When I finally made my way home, Margaret said that Allington had called, looking for me. I spent several minutes thinking up a plausible story and then phoned him at home. He seemed to accept what I said.

Does that matter, whether he believed what I said that night, or any other time? If I never meet Simon again, suspicions can do me no harm. My actions will be quite innocent.

Most days I can't bring myself to write in this because that would mean thinking, and I can't bear to think.

Would I have started, had I known it would be over so soon? Of course. The point is the usefulness of what I've done, the future, not my feelings. They don't matter one way or the other. I have to live with them, but they have no objective importance.

Each day I go through my duties like a robot, acting automatically, smiling automatically. Will this end and will I come back to life? What life? Can I do anything that matters?

I'm still being followed. Why?

I have to prepare some material on the relationship between Britain's position in NATO and the possibility of membership in the EEC. I hope I can lose myself in that.

Paranoid fantasy. Of course. Mad. Of course. I am only pursued by spectres of my own invention.

But where are the sane men? I said to Daniel that he must tell me how he managed, and he said it was a habit. His poetry was a habit. It seems to me that I've never met a sane man. Where are they all?

Better the company of my fantasies.

Finished that job. Now left empty. Work is the opiate of the religious classes. Too true to be good. I'm giddy. I'll go out for a walk.

I keep recalling that last interview, over two weeks ago now. Can I have been wrong? I think so only in my weak and sentimental moments. Fine feelings are a luxury.

Sometimes I try to lose those who are following me and find myself wandering lost through strange suburbs. I've come to think of the tube stations as some kind of salvation. As soon as I find one, I know where I am. But they always know where to find me when they want to start again. There's a temptation sometimes to buy a ticket for some distant place, New Zealand or Kenya, someplace I've never been and to get on an airplane, taking no luggage. That old bourgeois dream of the desert island, Robinson Crusoe alone with the wilderness, making a kingdom that is only his.

As I walked along the street today, I saw a child, just a baby, asleep in a carriage. I stopped in the middle of the street and stood looking at the sleeping child, thinking, no not thinking, just looking, just knowing the weakness and delight of the child. As I stood there, tears came to my eyes and began to run down my cheeks, but even when the child's mother came out of the shop and looked at me, I couldn't look away, only stood there looking at the child and trying to say something. As I remember now, the feeling comes back.

Days later. Latter days. Time is my enemy in this disease my life. Symptoms: continual depression of spirits, ingrown soulnail, primary and secondary erotomania, carcinoma of the politic glands.

Whenever I can, I leave the office and go across to the National Gallery. If I'm lucky I can find a kind of calm there. I walk across the room in front of Rembrandt's portrait of himself in his old age, and the eyes follow me. If I walk back and forth enough times, I start to feel that we're communicating, old Rembrandt and I, and that the fat sad face understands what I'm feeling.

Or I wander from room to room searching out the nudes and exploring the kind of lust that each creates in me, the vulgar sensual Rubens lust, the cold detached Lucas Cranach lust.

Will Simon get in touch with me? It's been so long now. I watch men as they pass me, waiting for some sign of recognition, for some message. Perhaps I should contact him? No.

I wait for a message. I run from those that follow.

Sometime they will get tired of their pursuit. Simon will know. He'll contact me.

Yesterday I got in touch with Simon, using the empty envelope that he'd told me to use only in an emergency. He hasn't called yet. I don't expect him to.

Outside. Like the keyhole where I watch Margaret. I can never. What nonsense I write. I'll lock this up in the file and not take it out again. Or burn it.

15

It was dark and strange. The body. Where was it? Was it really dead so quickly? His hands felt funny where they'd held the throat. And who was it that he'd killed? It seemed that he couldn't remember. He knew that he must do something with the body, but there was no body. It was dark and strange, and he could look around him now and think that maybe it had been a nightmare. He could no longer remember who it was or just what had happened, except that his mother had been there. But why had he choked someone and killed him?

Jake was awake now, lying in the dark and listening to the breathing of the girl beside him, yet still half convinced that there was a body somewhere in the room that he had killed.

He reached out and touched the girl's skin. It was hot under his fingers. His hand was on her side, and he could feel her breathing. He turned toward her and reached out with his other hand and began to rub it slowly over her breasts which moved in his fingers. She made a noise and starting to wake up, turned toward him. Their mouths moved together, and their legs intertwined. She was wet as she rubbed herself against his leg. She turned on her back, drawing him over on top of her.

Lying above her suddenly recalled the nightmare to Jake, the moment when he had been leaning over the body, pressing down with his two hands. The image would not leave him, and he couldn't lose himself in the girl, tried to disappear into sensation but couldn't, except for moments. He was glad, after the deep moaning sighs of her climax, to sink back down into sleep.

When Jake woke in the morning, he found the girl looking at him from where she lay beside him in the bed.

"You were sound asleep," she said.

She moved over and kissed him on the face. They lay close together.

"My god," she said, "I'm glad you came back here last night."

"So am I," Jake said. He wondered if he was lying.

"Want some coffee?"

"Wouldn't mind." Jake was still mumbling, half asleep.

The girl got out of bed naked and hurried across to the gas ring. She put on the kettle. As she turned back toward the bed, she saw that Jake was looking at her.

"I'm fat, aren't I," she said. "Fat and hairy."

"No," Jake said. "You look good."

She climbed into bed and snuggled against him to keep warm.

"I don't like the way I look," she said.

"Why not?"

"I'd like to be thin and smooth. I can't even keep clean here."

Jake held her close, stroking her back and hips.

"You look just fine," he said.

They made love again, slowly and gently, talking inarticulately into each other's mouths. It was so soft and slow that Jake seemed to lose his body, to no longer know what was his own body and what was hers, as if she penetrated him as he did her and what they were was only soft sound and the movement of flesh until the end that was like an old song, a long slow dying into a sensitivity so intense that they didn't dare move or speak. They listened to the kettle boil, both knowing that someone should get up and make the coffee but both too relaxed to really care.

Finally the girl got out of bed. She pulled on a pair of slacks and a sweater and shoved her feet into Jake's boots, then made the coffee. She brought Jake a cup and sat down on the edge of the bed with hers.

"I need a cigarette," Jake said. "Can you reach the makings out of my jacket pocket?"

She picked up the jacket and handed it to him, and Jake rolled himself a cigarette and lit it.

"Would you take me back with you?" the girl said.

"No money," Jake said. "All I've got is about fifteen pounds and a return ticket."

"I've still got my return ticket," she said.

"You could have gone back anytime."

"I couldn't get around to making the break. I'm a weakling."

"What do you want me to do?"

"Take me wherever you're going. Once I'm in Canada, you can always get rid of me. Just send me home."

Jake looked at the wall. He read a slogan. VEN-CEREMOS.

"Look," she said, "just forget I asked you. I can go back anytime."

Jake reached out and touched her hair.

"I'll let you know when I'm going back," he said. "If you still want to go, I could probably take you with me."

She nodded, but without looking at him.

"Hey," Jake said, "you know what I once saw written on a wall in a scruffy little room down on Spadina Avenue in Toronto? BE HAPPY. THE WORLD WILL LEARN TO LOVE YOU SOME-DAY. It had flowers drawn all around it."

"Is that funny?" she said.

"No," Jake said, "just something I thought of."

"I'm hungry," the girl said, "but I don't think there's anything to eat here."

"Want me to go out and get something?" Jake said.

"I'll go," the girl said. "I've got some clothes on."

"Be gentle with my boots."

"Sure will." She picked up a coat and headed out the door. Jake lay on his back and looked at the ceiling of the room. The paint was peeling off in little white flakes. He thought about taking the girl back with him and wondered if he did whether she'd expect to stay.

There was something relaxing about this girl, something easy and undemanding, but something that you might get tired of after a while. Like Hattersley, who'd come to take her for granted because she didn't challenge him. Jake wondered if he'd do the same.

He closed his eyes and lay quietly, not really thinking of anything until he heard the door open. He looked in that direction and saw Hattersley taking off his coat. Hattersley hadn't looked toward the bed yet.

"Good morning," Jake said.

Hattersley turned and looked at him.

"You're a pretty fast worker," he said. His eyes were angry, but he was keeping himself controlled. Jake found himself wondering what he should do next. He was a bit apprehensive about what Hattersley might do, but at the same time, he was tempted to laugh. Hattersley filled the kettle and put it on the gas ring.

"Where is she?" he said.

"She went out to get some food."

Hattersley sat down in a chair, picked up a newspaper and began looking through it. He wasn't really reading anything. Jake wondered if he should get up, put his clothes on and leave. He wasn't sure he was cool enough to pull it off. Besides Lucy had his boots, and he wasn't going to walk out barefoot. That wouldn't be cool at all.

The kettle started to boil, and Hattersley stood up and made himself a cup of coffee. He didn't offer Jake one.

It was getting harder every minute for Jake to lie there saying nothing. He glanced over at Hattersley who was sitting down with his coffee.

"Maybe you could fuck off now," Hattersley said. "Or are you staying?"

"She's got my boots," Jake said.

Hattersley went back to his newspaper. There was a long silence, then a noise as Lucy came in. She was carrying two or three small bags of groceries, which she put down on a chair. She looked at the two of them.

"Hi Donny," she said to Hattersley. "How's it going down there?"

He looked at her for a long time before he spoke.

"They're threatening to have a court order by tomorrow and put them out, but we had some television people there, and that makes the councillors fucking nervous."

"Are you hungry?" she said.

He shrugged.

146

She took out a package of biscuits and opened them, then took a piece of cheese and cut it up. She put them on a plate and handed them to Hattersley.

"I asked Jake to take me back with him," she said.

Hattersley stood up. He picked up the cheese and biscuits from the plate and put them in the pocket of his coat.

"Maybe you could let me know when you're leaving," he said and walked out. Lucy stood staring at the wall.

"Shit," she said, "why did it have to happen this way?" She walked to the bed, sat down and put her face on Jake's chest.

"I'm an awful bitch, aren't I?" she said. "I'm a real shit."

Jake put his arms around her.

"It had to happen sometime," he said. "He'll blame me, not you."

The girl lifted her face and looked at him.

"I can't stay here now," she said. "Can I stay with you?"

"She doesn't know whether my brother's alive or dead," Jake said. "I can't take you there."

The girl moved away from him and stood up.

"When are you going back home?" she said.

"I don't know," Jake said. "I wish to hell I did."

16

I don't really know how I got here. When I looked across the square from just outside the door, I sensed that there was someone waiting for me, and after a few minutes' observation, I saw him. Once again the first thought was that I must escape, but I couldn't think where to go.

I stood there too long. Everyone else was moving. Everyone but the two of us. The big black cabs went past like a horde of beetles racing away from a fire. Those on foot watched and ran. I knew that the longer I stood there, the worse it was. I walked down the steps. There seemed no hope of getting a cab on the corner so I began to walk up to Charing Cross Road where I thought it might be easier. I suppose I assumed then that I was going home.

It's over a week now since I've been able to drive. I can't do it.

Does Margaret imagine where I am? How could she? Imagine this room, faded cream and green, the bed, one closet, the single table against the wall where I'm writing this. The sink.

When I came in, I lay down on the bed and closed my eyes and thought of empty things. I started to wonder if they'd know I was here and that led me back.

What time did I get on the tube? It was after dark. I saw him again, and I walked around a corner and down an alley, then ran the length of the alley and came out near a tube station. As I hurried in, I got a ticket from a machine and went down a long escalator, walking down so fast I nearly lost my balance, then when I reached the bottom, I got on the other escalator going back up, standing still this time as the underground wind swept past me, and watching. I thought I saw one of them on the escalator coming down, but he couldn't cross over to me.

When I reached the top, there was a tunnel to another line, and I followed that, running, and caught a train just as it was about to leave. I changed trains several times, once going far into the suburbs and walking away from the station before turning back and taking another train.

What of the journals in my files at home? They must be destroyed. This too.

If they could be kept somewhere, locked up in a vault for twenty-five or thirty years until after my death and Margaret's death, they could be taken out then as historical documents. Someone should know what this has meant to me.

There are footsteps in the halls. Shouting that echoes in the distance. Across the hall is a bathroom with a tub and toilet. I'd like to have a bath, but the tub looks dirty.

Margaret will never understand, perhaps never know.

If I defected, I could offer something, I suppose, as an expert on Canadian affairs. Would they use me?

Who is Simon? He must be an illegal here in England, but why would he work with me? Doesn't that put some risk on their whole illegal network? At first, the other man, from the embassy, then Simon. Who is he? Who does he work for? I know nothing.

I should phone Margaret and make some excuse. What will I do in the morning? I could phone the office and tell them I'm sick.

How long can I stay here? I don't think he believed my story about just arriving in London and losing my bags. How long will they let me stay? I could get a bed-sitter somewhere.

If I have given myself to them, I must give myself entirely. Trust them. I have given myself to the future, I must put myself in their hands.

Why don't they tell me what they want? I'd like to talk to Simon and ask him for an explanation. Would he explain anything or just tell me to trust him and wait. As always.

I'm so tired. It was strange to wake up in the tube

and not know how far I'd travelled or where I was, just to wake up and see the two young girls across the aisle looking at me. One had very big breasts, and I could imagine them in my hands, just in that second of waking and seeing her there, it was as if they were actually in my hands. The sensation made me quiver. There were a couple of workmen in the car and an unhealthy old woman. The girls were cheaply dressed. I wondered where I was until the train came into the station.

I've never been here before. I was so tired and con-fused at first that I just stood on the platform. The station smelled of age and smoke, and a big gouge had been torn out of the wall across from me.

When I got into the street, there was a sex movie, and I thought of going in there.

Fortunate I took the street I did. I might have walked all night, unable to think of where to go. This is a shelter of sorts, a defence against a decision really. Until morning.

EVENING PRAYERS IN THE CHAPEL IN EIGHT MINUTES TIME.

Echoing.

I'll skip evening prayers tonight. God can take care of himself.

The woman wasn't really a dwarf, didn't have the big head and disproportioned legs, but was fifty or more, and the size of a child. She came into the café where I went to get a sandwich. I just remembered her now, the way she stared at me until I was convinced that she was one of them, sent to watch me.

Or a messenger, an angel.

I felt better after the food. She was still staring. I suppose she is sensitive about her size and stares aggressively to put others on the defensive.

How I wish I could get in touch with Simon. What if he said to go back to work and be my normal self? That they would have no more work for me because I was too jittery. Then suddenly I would be what I appear, a respectable Canadian foreign-service officer of the middle rank. Could I bear to be what I appear to be? Truth can be the greatest of all lies.

There are messages, the girl on the train, her breasts in my hands, the little old woman, there is an echo of their presence, but it is often broken. Men might be angels, each a messenger to all those he meets. Someday there will be more light on the faces of men.

How beautiful are the feet of them that preach the gospel of peace. I remember as a boy sitting in church and listening to someone sing that. I think I looked at the minister's feet to see if there was light shining around them.

Why the feet? Because they are messengers, I suppose, like Mercury with his winged feet.

Do the feet of a man show his character?

The old woman and the girl brought me the message of their *presence*. In the new world this *presence* will light up every contact between men.

Often it seems so far away, and the steps toward it so small. What have I done? Passed on a bit of information, peripheral at best. Photographed documents that were hardly worth reading. I'm not the source they need.

I can hear from outside the noise of cars passing. So much movement to no purpose, men burning with their greeds and lusts and fears. The one possible justification of capitalism is the energy it releases, the way greed and fear set a man on fire and send him out into the streets. The world is on fire with this terrible energy. It's the fire that burns Vietnam.

151

In the new world the energy will be controlled, used.

EVENING PRAYERS IN THE CHAPEL IN TWO
MINUTES.

Why do I write that down? It seems to matter, the
anonymous voice echoing in the halls. I suppose it's
the man I met when I came in. He knew there was
something wrong about me and tried to put me off
by saying he was just the night man and couldn't rent
me a room. But he changed his mind.

Margaret, what shall I do about her? Can I go back?

I went out of my room just now and downstairs looking
for a phone. The halls are dark and narrow, and when
I got to the end, I couldn't get the lift to work. I
looked up and down into the little cage, but there was
no sign of the lift, so I walked down the stairway, circling round and round the lift cage as I went and coming
out on a floor where the teenagers that fill this place
were having some kind of dance. They stared at me
wondering that a man my age and dressed like this
should be here.

I saw a sign pointing to the telephones in the basement and went down the stairs. Two young couples
were going into the billiard room. There are two
telephones there, but they aren't enclosed in any way.
How could I stand beside a West Indian who's arguing
with someone about some flat they're planning to rent
and try to convince Margaret that I'm calling from my
office?

I couldn't talk there, not to anyone. Maybe later
when everyone is asleep. I'm tired, but I don't want to
sleep.

On the way back up, walking slowly up the endless
steps to the fourth floor, I saw a man, an oriental,
standing on one of the landings watching me through

the glass door. I began to speculate again and was glad to be back here locked in this room. It's a kind of safety.

I have the power to check on myself. I didn't say that the man was watching me deliberately, was sent to watch me, only that he watched me and that I was frightened. I've been part of a world where strange things happen.

Could I inflict pain if it was necessary?

Puzzling. The lost time earlier. I was in a pub, or several, maybe I drank too much, I remember being sick or faint and everyone staring at me, different people, a lot of sideburns and moustaches and clothes of odd colours. The little old woman staring in through the door. But was she? Or at the café where I had a sandwich. She couldn't be at both.

There's no-one following me. It's just nerves. At worst I could be found out, but what could they prove? I could resign. There's no-one following me.

Do I know anything that is a threat to Simon? I can only identify him by sight. My bit of information would only be useful to someone with other information. He has a strange accent, almost American, but with many British idioms. I suppose a skilful police officer could make something of that.

I looked out the window at the boys and girls laughing in the yard below, hardly more than children. Blind unaware helpless children, how can they know what the world is? That the real wars are fought in the minds of the hungry, the victims. These are victims too, but don't know it. Someday they'll look back, perhaps remember this night or some other and think that many things were possible but are no longer possible, and they'll wonder who's to blame. I envy their ignorance. To see things, but to be unable to make more than one step, is too painful. Pain.

The city reaches out for miles from here, buildings low to the ground, a contained unhappiness not like the soaring bright paranoia of New York. People all wound in the threads of their commitments, children, houses, friends, jobs. What I might have been if the child hadn't died.

There's a man standing out by the street, not moving, just watching.

Would they kill me? I watched him out there from behind a corner of the curtain. He didn't move or appear to speak to those that passed him, only waited. What patience he must have. I'd like to have that kind of patience, to wait, just wait.

I looked at myself in the dirty mirror above the sink. It was a strange sensation, like being drunk and catching a glimpse of oneself in a mirror looking much the same as ever while inside being a different person. My face is the same round bland thing, tired and unshaven, but still the face I've lived my life with. Why do I think I should have a face to go with the role I'm playing, since the essence of the role is secrecy? Where is the difference in me? In my soul if I have one?

Or in my history? That's it, I suppose. I've written my own history instead of letting circumstance write that history for me. I've made history into freedom.

I'm not bound by what I own, by what I've been, not even by the fear of what will happen next. I don't need to feel that the world tomorrow will be as safe as the world today. That's a kind of freedom.

Tired.

Middle of the night now, My watch has stopped. I lay down on the bed and fell asleep. Terrible nightmare. I was riding on the tube, and Margaret was riding in the next car. I could see her there. She was with a man who was undressing her. She lay there moaning with desire. Everyone in the car was looking away from them or making remarks about how it should be stopped. When he took his penis out of his trousers, it was very big and entirely covered with black hair. Then the train was dark, and I was suffocating, but each time we came to a station it was lighted, and I could see Margaret on the platform with a man. She was naked, but he had all his clothes on. Then the train went on without ever stopping, and I was suffocating again. The train went faster and faster until I could only catch a glimpse of them as we went past.

Then Simon was in the dream. We had a signal for meeting, but I couldn't remember it, and he stood there on the platform waiting for me to get off the train, but I didn't want to get off until I'd remembered the signal. The train started to pull out of the station, and I was running to the door when I woke up.

For a long time, I couldn't make myself get off the bed. I looked over here at the pile of papers, and I wanted to burn them, but I couldn't get off the bed. I closed my eyes, but I could feel the nightmare coming back so I forced myself to get up. I came over to the desk intending to burn all this, but when I sat down I realized that I had no matches. After sitting here a few minutes, I started to write again. I don't know why I write everything down, except that there's nothing else to do. Writing it calms me down a little.

I went to the window and carefully looked past the curtain. He's still there, sitting in a car now, on the other side of the street, but still waiting. I'm starting to get hungry, but I don't want to unlock the door.

I've been out of the room. I walked up and down the dark halls as quietly as I could, going through each hallway on each floor. Sometimes I could hear snoring behind a door, and I'd stop and listen, fascinated. I found a vending machine on the second floor that made tea or hot chocolate but had no cups. I walked further looking in washrooms until I found a plastic cup someone had left there. Went back to the machine and got watery chocolate so hot it hurt my hand as I carried it back up to my room. When I opened the door from the staircase to this floor, there was a man standing in the hall. He nodded to me and let himself into his room. I had to put the hot chocolate down to get out my key and open the door. Good to be back in here with the door locked. I keep touching my pocket to make sure that the key is still there.

When I was wandering through the halls, I thought of going down to the basement and phoning Margaret, but I knew I'd have to pass by the office. Someone might have seen me.

Those kids out in the yard. Did they feel destruction hanging over their heads? Huge shining rockets that can deliver a disaster in seconds. There's a certain kind of madness that can love them.

The last days. *Dies irae* is our anthem. Think of the innocence of my childhood when I could imagine heroes. Think. Don't think.

There's so little time. The slow boring day by day deceives us into thinking that time is slow. Time is dead. There is only now.

The Chinese, the blacks, the poor, history belongs to them now. They're hungry enough to eat the fire we live in, breathe it, take their nourishment from it, grow on it.

There's nothing behind the face in the mirror, should be nothing. I can't afford to have a self. Must be inert, like the key I use to open this locked door.

I think now of the man I was in Bonn when I met her, touched her. As if I'd been waiting for that. I'd like her to know what has become of me.

He is as hard as Stalin, I can see that in his eyes when he looks at me, assessing me and my information, trying to fathom how he could get more and better material.

Imagine an invisible wall. Everything's like a drawing in two dimensions with no chance for the third, that changes the whole pattern, makes a new world. The new man is an angel. Only afterward is it possible to understand this.

Too much thinking.

I think I slept again for a few minutes, but it was not restful sleep. Frantic with nightmares. Simon was chasing me, shouting that I'd forgotten everything important he'd ever told me, that I'd got it all wrong. He kept using that CIA jargon. *Terminate with extreme prejudice.* I kept asking him what they had said, whether there wasn't a place for me. But he just went on shouting those words. *Terminate with extreme prejudice, terminate with extreme terminate with extreme prejudice.*

The man outside is still there, sitting in his car. Why can't they see that what I've done is right?

I've carried the quotation in my wallet for months. It's small help.

Finally, when the class war is about to be fought to a finish, disintegration of the ruling class and the old order of society becomes so active, so acute, that a small part of the ruling

class breaks away to make common cause with the revolutionary
class, the class that holds the future in its hands.

What does that mean?

Almost morning.

I remember once staying out with friends for most of the night, coming in when it had started to get light, still a bit drunk but starting to get sober, walking in my stocking feet to be quiet. As I walked past my father's study, the door was open, and I saw him in there, reading. He saw me and told me to come in. I thought he was going to be angry with me. He looked angry, but then he always did.

"Do you have to go to school today?" he said.

I told him that I didn't. That the school was closed for a teacher's convention. He just nodded. He went back to reading his book, one of the old Russian books that filled his days now.

I can get breakfast downstairs after seven o'clock, but I feel as if I were beyond the need of food, halfway to some new state.

Perhaps I'm dead. Or perhaps I have only begun to live.

Margaret will be waking soon, going to run her bath, undressing only behind a closed door where I have watched her so many times.

Later.

17

Jake walked through the doors of Canada House and went straight to the elevator. The receptionist was watching him and started to say something, but Jake climbed into the elevator without waiting to hear her. He had to do something definite about John and send some message to his mother. So far he'd been floundering, unable to find any information that meant anything. He knew nothing more than what his mother could read in the newspapers.

Jake had thought about going to the hostel where the papers had been found, to see if he could learn anything there, if John had said anything that might indicate where he was now. More and more Jake felt that his brother was dead, his body gone somewhere under the Thames. Perhaps in another few days it would start to decompose and come to the surface.

The hall was empty as he walked toward Allington's office. Jake reached the two doors, one that led into the secretary's office and one that led directly into Allington's room. He knocked at Allington's private door. In the same moment both doors opened. Allington stood at one and his young blonde secretary at the other.

"That's all right, Erna," Allington said. "I'll look after this."

He stood back to let Jake walk into his office. Then he closed the door.

"I didn't expect to see you again," he said.

"It's your lucky week," Jake said. "I said I'd be back."

Allington sat down.

"Did you talk to The Man?" Jake said.

"I don't know what you're talking about."

"You said you'd ask the High Commissioner whether I could see some of the journal."

"I told you what he'd say."

"Now tell me what he did say."

"He said no, of course."

"Why?"

"I don't have to give you any reasons."

"Don't you?"

Allington shook his head.

"That's the last word, eh?"

"I hope so."

Jake looked at the man sitting behind the desk. He was fiddling with some papers, trying to give Jake the idea that he was busy and should be left alone.

"Listen," Jake said. "Tell me what you think of what my brother did."

"No. I don't have to answer your questions."

"I know you don't have to. But just tell me. Your good deed for the day."

"For God's sake go away. You bore me."

"You amuse me. Almost as good as the movies, except I can talk back. Tell me what you think of my brother. Or tell me why you don't become a spy."

"I can have you put out if you make it necessary."

"That might be amusing too. Shit, that might be fun."

"Go away. I won't discuss it any more, and I won't hesitate to call the police for more than another minute."

"ok, I don't want to make your blood pressure any worse. Just two little things and I'll go."

"What?"

"First, will you give me the address of the place where they found his briefcase."

Allington lifted the phone and asked his secretary to find the address. He put down the phone.

160

"Well, what's the other thing?"

He had a long-suffering look on his face.

"Can I screw your secretary before I go?"

Allington's face started to get red, and he was about to speak when the secretary knocked at the door and walked in with a slip of paper. Allington didn't know where to look, but Jake smiled at the girl and she smiled back. She handed Allington the paper and went back out of the room. When the door closed behind her, Allington held the paper out to Jake.

"I don't want to see you here again," he said. "Next time I'll call the police."

Jake took the paper. He was tired of being in the office now. The whole thing seemed stupid and futile.

"Thanks for everything," he said and walked out. When he got back downstairs, he read the address. It was completely unfamiliar to him, a place called Stockwell Road in a southern postal district, so he decided to take a cab. It seemed a legitimate way to spend his mother's money, although he doubted if the trip would lead to much.

He managed to hail a cab and handed the driver the slip of paper, then sat back in the leather seat and waited as the cab drove on. He thought again of what he was going to tell his mother. Perhaps the simplest thing would be to make up whatever story was likely to be most comforting to her and tell her that. He could say that they knew John was alive in Russia, but nobody wanted to let on, and it would never be publicly admitted. As long as no body turned up, that story would do. She'd have the comfort of thinking John was alive, but wouldn't expect to hear from him. Jake decided that if he couldn't find anything in the next couple of days, he'd phone and tell his mother that.

The cab moved on through unfamiliar districts south of the river. Jake looked at the pigeons sitting like lumps of dirt on the roof of a building they were passing and took out his little notebook to write a fragment of a poem.

> A bird shit on your head
> and you complained.
> Do you think you're somebody important?

He read it over a couple of times, quite pleased with it, and then put away the notebook. A couple of minutes later the cab stopped at a big red brick building. Jake paid the driver and went in the front door.

Near the door was a counter separating the hallway from a small office, and inside the office a man was counting piles of change. Jake stood at the counter and waited for the man to finish counting the money and look up. It took him a long time. He kept changing his mind about which pile to put the coins in, and each time he did that he'd have to start over again counting them. He was a small man, and his suit coat and pants looked as if he'd worn them for a long time. He finally noticed Jake and came to the counter.

"What can I do for you?"

"My name's Jake Martens."

"You can't get a room until eleven o'clock, you know. Otherwise we can't keep the records properly."

"No, I don't want a room."

"Well then, what can I do for you?"

"I think my brother stayed here one night last week. You might have read about him in the papers. He was at the Canadian High Commission."

"The spy?"

Jake nodded.

"I told the police everything. Gave them what he'd left here."

He stopped.

"Just go on. Tell me the rest."

"Nothing to tell. He came in and took the room. Next day the woman went in to do up the room and found

162

his things. She came to me and said I'd told her 416 was empty. I said it was, he'd made no arrangements for another night. There's a notice in every room, you can't miss it, says you've to be out by ten or tell me you're coming back. And pay in advance. So I said to her that he hadn't said a word to me, but she said he'd left a load of papers and a bag. I said she could bring them to me, and I'd hold them here in case he came back."

"What was in the papers?"

"Well, I wouldn't know that, would I?"

"You might."

"It wasn't my business to be reading them."

"How did you know where to phone about them?"

He was caught off balance and paused for a second.

"That was later, when I thought he wasn't coming back. I just had a quick look and saw right off that he was using paper from your High Commissioner's Office, and I said to myself I'd better ring them up about it. It was a surprise when the CID men came. I was just going off then, finished for the day, when they came in."

"What did they ask you?"

"Just what you'd expect. It's all been in the papers, all that sort of thing."

A teenage boy came up to the counter, and the man turned away from Jake, who was tempted to walk away and give up but decided to stay and give it another try. The boy finished his business and left. The man turned back to Jake.

"I don't know what there is to tell you."

"Were you here when he came in?"

"It was nearly time for me to leave when he came too. I'd been on from two till ten, and the next day I was changing and going on from six till two. That was when the police came, just on two."

"What time did my brother come in?"

"That's what I say, it would have been close on ten because I was ready to leave. I'd started to think that the other man might be late. Your brother came in and said he wanted a room. I thought it was a bit funny, coming in at that time without any proper luggage, but we had some empty rooms so I put him in 416. He seemed a bit odd, I suppose. Nothing you could put a finger on. Tired."

"Did anyone come to see him?"

"I wouldn't know that. I was off at ten and not back until six. I was a few minutes late too, though I'm not often."

"Who was here after ten?"

"Well, it was the other man, of course, wasn't it? He didn't ever say anything about anyone coming to see him. Of course, how would he know? There are so many people in and out."

"Did you see my brother leave?"

"No. I said to the police that was a funny thing, that neither of us saw him leave. Neither one of us." He shook his head. "If I were you, I should talk to the Special Branch or to the people at your High Commission."

"I talked to someone at the High Commission."

"Was he helpful?"

"No."

"Why is it you're so interested? Just because he was your brother?"

"That's right. I haven't seen him for a couple of years, and I'm curious. And my mother is worried and wants to know what's going on."

"Well he'll likely be off to Russia with the rest of that lot, won't he? Old Philby and his friends. Rotten lot of traitors, I'd call them."

"I guess they had their reasons."

"Thought they were a bit too good for the rest of us. Too many around like that who think they know everything."

164

"Well, thanks anyway," Jake said.

The man nodded and went back to his pile of money. Jake read the date on the calendar over his head. It was familiar.

"I hope your money turns out right for you," Jake said.

"I shall go on until it does," the man said.

Jake turned to walk out, trying again to think why the date on the calendar had seemed important, and before he'd reached the outside door, he remembered that it was the day of the Action Group's sit-in. He worked out what time it was in Canada. It was still night there, several hours yet before time for the sit-in. Jake decided that he should send them a telegram. As he walked along the street, he tried to think of the best way of wording it. He decided to say BEST WISHES TO THE REVOLUTION VENCEREMOS LOVE JAKE. That seemed all right.

As he walked toward the tube station, keeping his eyes open for a Post Office from which he could send a wire, Jake noticed a car pull up to the pavement beside him. His friend from the restaurant. Old funny-eyes.

Jake decided to be difficult and not stop. He walked on down the street, and the car continued beside him, pulling a little ahead and stopping so the man could open the driver's door and speak to him.

"Mr. Martens."

"Yes," Jake said. He didn't move toward the car.

"Could I speak to you?"

"Sure," Jake said. He still didn't move toward the car. They were nearly ten feet away from each other, and there was traffic going by so it wasn't easy for the man to make himself heard.

"Why don't you get in the car?" the man said.

"All right," Jake said. He walked across to the car. The door was locked, and the man reached across

165

from his side of the seat and opened it. Jake got in and sat down. The man put the car in gear and pulled forward a few feet to a corner, then turned left into a side street and drove along the street to a square of big, half-run-down houses. He pulled into the curb and turned off the engine.

"Well," he said. "What do you hear of your brother?"

"Probably not as much as you do."

"You think not?"

"The newspapers are getting bored with the subject."

"Of course."

The man reached into his pocket and took out a package of cigarettes. He offered one to Jake, who took one and allowed the man to light it for him. It felt strange to be smoking a filter tip.

He inhaled the smoke and said nothing.

"This is an odd corner of the city to find you in."

"You too."

"I was here watching you."

"And you know why I'm here."

"Do I?"

"If you read the newspapers."

"What do they say?"

"That the hostel is the last place my brother was seen."

"And are they right?"

"What do you think?"

The man shrugged.

Jake took a drag on his cigarette and sat in silence. The game of seeing who could let on the least amused him a little, but he was aware of it as pointless.

"Why do you keep asking to talk to me when you have nothing to say?" Jake said.

"Perhaps I have nothing to say because you have nothing to say."

"If I tell you something, you'll tell me something, is that it?"

"I would certainly do my best. After all we're both interested in your brother."

"But not in the same way."

"We both wish to help him."

Jake took another mouthful of smoke and inhaled it.

"Let's stop this game," he said. "Just what do you want? To know what I know about John? To be perfectly truthful, I think it'd be silly to tell you anything I might happen to know. Because I don't trust you."

"You trust the police and the people at Canada House?"

"Maybe not, but I know what they want."

"What's that?"

"To put my brother in jail."

The man butted his cigarette in the ashtray under the dashboard.

"Are you sure of that?"

Jake didn't answer.

"In a way," the man said, "it's a matter of public relations now. Your brother is no longer any use to them or to me, really. Except as a way of making a point."

Jake felt that this should be the truth, that he ought to believe the man but he didn't, and he wondered if he was being foolishly defensive.

"I'd like to have you help me," the man said. "From what I've been able to learn about you, I thought you might be willing to help."

It was tempting. It was as if the man had drawn a line and dared Jake to step across it into a different, more exciting world. The world of his nightmares, a place where everything was clear. Just step over the line, just once. Prove you can.

"Right now, believe me, I want to help your brother, and later on, there might be other things. You're bright enough and independent enough that I'd like to have you available."

167

Jake said nothing, only looked out the window of the car and along the empty street.

"Are you short of money?" the man said. "The trip must have been expensive."

"You'd pay me?"

"I have a certain amount of money available."

"Did you pay John?"

The man took out the package of cigarettes and held it toward Jake, who shook his head. The man took out a cigarette and lit it, then turned back toward Jake. He smiled, and Jake suddenly realized very clearly that he didn't like this man. The man was cunning and wanted to invade him. Jake wouldn't trust him, wouldn't offer him anything but silence.

"I've thought about it," Jake said, "and what I think is that I'm not interested. Now or ever. Maybe I'm making a mistake, but I can live with that." He opened the car door. "I don't much want to go through this again," he said. "We don't have any more words to say." He got out of the car. After a few seconds, the man started the engine and moved away down the street.

Jake watched the car drive away, getting smaller in the distance of the city street, then turning a corner and leaving the street empty. Even when it was gone, he stood there. Wondered now if maybe he'd made the wrong choice, copped out. That car was his transport for a nightmare trip that he'd been living in the back of his head for years, and he'd handed back the ticket.

He turned and walked to the end of the street. Stopped. Looked back. As if there would be something back there, his own shadow, the shadow of the car, as if he would see the whole scene replayed in the empty air like a movie. The overture to a nightmare sequence.

Nearby Jake saw a public playground where a group of small children were riding a roundabout. There was a woman watching the children play, sitting on a bench and watching them. She wore a brown coat.

168

Simple things: children, a roundabout, a man who stood on the street and watched them. Jake had copped out on the nightmare trip. John had taken it.

18

I think this is the eighth day that I've been here. For the last two things have been a little different, and this morning, suddenly, everything changed. When I woke up, the first thing I noticed was that I was hungry, and when I got out of bed and looked out the window, I knew that everything was different now.

When I went out to eat, I bought this notebook and a pen, for I felt that I must record this change that has taken place in me.

As I sit here at this little writing desk and look at the bed, I keep remembering those first days when I lay there hour after hour with blankets on and my coat, and the covers drawn up over my head so that I could disappear into dark and silence. Sometimes a woman would come and knock on the door, wanting to clean and make the bed, and I'd tell her to go away, that I was busy. And I was. Busy nourishing myself on dark and sleep.

I'm surprised that the manageress didn't phone the police. I suppose she was accustomed to strange behaviour, and I paid for a week in advance and gave her extra money to see that I wasn't disturbed.

The last bits of my cunning went into the approach to her. I went to a barber and got shaved, bought a small case and concocted the story about the work I had to do without disturbance. I remember climbing the stairs to this room, aware that I was reaching the last resources of my mind, concentrating to keep from starting to scream or collapsing and falling down stairs. Then I reached the room and locked the door behind me. I took off my clothes and got into the bed. It was cold, but at first I didn't have the energy to get up and put on more blankets. Finally I did get up and put on all the blankets I could find and a coat on top of them and got back into the bed and didn't stir.

At first I slept, then started to wake with nightmares, the same ones over and over again with Margaret and Simon. When I'd wake after a nightmare, I'd search for some comforting thought to lead me back toward sleep. It was hard, at first, to find the right thing. Most of the things would draw me back toward the past, toward memories that I wasn't yet strong enough to sustain. Finally, I found a perfect method. I'd imagine that I was an animal, a sort of groundhog, but nothing that specific, just something small and furry and brown curled up in the darkness under the earth. I'd imagine the layers of earth above me and the snow that was above that, but I wouldn't imagine the light shining on the snow. When I reached the snow, I'd start back down through all the whiteness of the snow, then the earth with roots and larvae buried there, then myself passing the winter.

I'd listen to the beat of my heart and concentrate on slowing it the way an animal's heartbeat slows during hibernation. As I concentrated on slowing my heartbeat, I'd fall asleep, and the hours would pass.

When I had to get up to relieve myself, it was painful to move about, to see the dull walls and old furniture, to think that perhaps I ought to eat. But I'd get back into bed, remembering that hibernating animals don't need to eat, that the slow winter body could live on its fat, and I'd fall asleep again.

After the first couple of days, things began to change. The nightmares came less often. It was easier to lie awake now and then, still thinking of myself as the animal, but quietly concentrating on slowing my heartbeat, even when sleep wouldn't come.

One afternoon I got up to empty my bladder and found myself staggering when I walked. I decided that I must go out and get some food.

It took me a long time to sort out my clothes and put them on. It seemed as if I'd never seen such things as clothes before. I'd stare at a shoe and feel that it was somehow impossible to put it on my foot. For a long time I'd look at the odd black leather object, then I'd put my foot toward it, and the accustomed motions would take place, and the shoe would be on. Then I stared at it because it had to be tied and that too seemed impossible.

I think it probably took me an hour or more to dress myself. I was afraid that I'd stagger or fall down the stairs as I went out, but I managed to walk to the street and along the street until I found a grocer's shop, where I bought a loaf of bread. There was nothing else that I could think of, and even now I wasn't hungry, just felt that I must eat to stay alive.

I brought the bread back to my room. Put a shilling in the gas meter and lit the fire. I was cold after being outside, and I thought it would be easier to eat the bread if I toasted it by the gas fire. I still wasn't hungry, and I was sure that the bread would stick in my throat.

I burnt my fingers trying to toast the piece of bread, but managed to eat some by tearing it in small pieces. Then I got back into bed. It was easy to sleep. I was tired after being out for the first time.

I slept and woke and slept and woke. Once or twice as I lay awake in the bed, I began to think. About

171

Simon or about Margaret. I wondered what Simon would be doing, if he had seen stories about me in the papers, if he was looking for me. That was a dangerous track for my thoughts to follow, and I had to bring them back, control them, be the animal again.

Remembering Margaret troubled me, but in a safer way. I must have caused her pain and I regretted that, but my mind could think of nothing that I could do that would help. I kept thinking that I should send her a letter, tell her that I'm all right. But am I? Now it seems I am. Everything is simple now.

Today I can even think of Simon again. I'm sure he won't bother to harm me. I'm not important enough for that. There's still a nagging doubt in my mind when I write that, but I do believe that it's true, that I have nothing to fear. To know that is a beginning.

It's strange, but I've started to feel hungry again, though it's not long since I went out and had a big breakfast. I suppose it's the accumulated hunger of the last week. When I look in the mirror, my clothes seem too big for me. I must have lost a lot of weight during the week.

Strange too that I've spent a week in this room, yet it seems unfamiliar. I just noticed a picture of some kind of blue flower hanging on the wall beside the wardrobe, and it was the first time I'd seen it. Until today I was here but not really here.

This morning when I stood at the window, aware of my hunger, aware that something had changed, I saw the people passing by on the street below me on their way to work, a milkman passing in his electric truck, stopping to deliver milk at each door, and I was surprised. It seems a strange word, but that was exactly the feeling I had, as if it were the most unexpected thing in the world to see a man delivering milk, to see pigeons on the pavement, to see a man striding quickly past with a briefcase.

172

I got too hungry, went out and bought a box of chocolates, and now I'm sitting here with the chocolates in front of me, eating them one at a time.

As I was paying for the chocolates, I noticed how little of my money was left, and for a moment I was worried, wondering what I'd do when it was gone, but the worry was soon over. Today will see the resolution, the conclusion of it all. It's quite simple.

When I was walking back from the store I saw a policeman, and without thinking, I turned a corner to avoid him, but when I'd done that, I was almost sorry. It would have been interesting to walk past him and see if he recognized me, stopped me. There must have been pictures circulated.

The first days, when the newspapers would have been full of speculation, I was never out of here, so I haven't seen what they said, but I can imagine it. There's a certain ritual to journalism. While I was out I bought a newspaper, but when I look at it now, it seems hardly worth my attention. Everything so obvious, so hollow. Less than real, like my own former actions when I remember them. They're like the actions of a character in a story that I'd read or imagined. Or written. Made it up and circumstance had accommodated me with some kinds of accidents. But I always knew that. But now it's as if I'd written that story about some other man and now it was finished and another story was waiting to be written. The first one just needs an ending, but that will be simple.

Sitting here, I've deliberately tried to recall what I wrote and said before, and I can see how important it all was to me then, but it's all in a different language. But I won't deny the man that I was. He acted for the best, for the future. He was visited by angels.

I've finished the chocolates.

I wonder what prison will be like. The idea is appealing. Once again, so simple and quiet. *Freedom is a bourgeois illusion.* If so, to go to prison is to be deprived of an illusion, to discover truth. And a certain humility which is appealing too. I wonder if they'll teach me a trade.

What of Margaret? She'll be able to live modestly on our savings and on what she inherited from her father. Perhaps she'll come and visit me sometimes. Will it matter to her that I'm in prison?

I suppose I'll be extradited and tried in Canada, but they'll question me here first. I wonder if they've read the journals? That's a disturbing thought because they won't really understand them at all. But I suppose that doesn't matter. They'll serve their purpose, provide the necessary conspiracy, since Lucifer the always-necessary conspiracy. I am the necessary enemy.

Being in prison couldn't be all that different from being here in this room. Accept the routine, and everything is simple. It's more puzzling to imagine the end of my sentence and wonder what I'll do then. Foolish to anticipate.

How much longer shall I wait here? I don't seem quite ready yet. The time will come and I'll know it.

It's afternoon now. I went out and ate lunch at a restaurant near here. It took nearly all my money, and I deliberately spent the rest, the last few shillings, on a paperback. I didn't want it, just wanted to be rid of the last of the money, to know that I had nothing. As I walked back here, my pockets were empty, and I felt happy and free.

Not long now. I can tell that the time is coming closer, as if I were waiting for some event, an important meeting, and watching the clock until it was time to leave. There's no clock here, yet I know the time is coming close.

I'll see Margaret again. What will I tell her? There should be some way to tell her so that she'll understand. Perhaps she already does. What can I tell her except that I did what was necessary, gave what little I had to offer to those who seem, however imperfectly, to have a grip on the future?

Words are so inadequate.

What can I ever say to my mother? Nothing, except that I hope she's well, that I regret any pain I've caused her.

I don't like to remember my mother and my father, myself when I was young. I don't know why, but there's something uneasy about those memories. I think of my father and imagine his eyes looking at me from so far away, as they always did, seeing everything and loving nothing in the whole world. A man without hope or faith of any kind, facing emptiness night after night.

Dangerous memories. Better to think of the prison, confession, the trial, all the simple things. The ending of one story, the beginning of another in a different language, a different time.

I stood looking out the window, watching the people below, so busy on their way. The time is coming closer, and suddenly I felt a temptation to climb back in the bed, to be the animal again. That's why I had to be rid of all the money, so that I couldn't give in to that.

19

Jake opened the door of the police station where he was to see his brother. All the way down he'd been trying to plan what he should say, but even as he walked up the steps into the station he was aware that he hadn't found the words. He still couldn't quite believe that John would appear and talk to him. Even though Margaret had already seen him and spoken to him it didn't seem possible. Jake suddenly had the feeling that he wouldn't recognize John. He tried to remember his face.

He walked up to the wooden counter in the room just off the hall. The room was painted in a strange mixture of different browns as if it had been done by a group of wholly independent painters, each determined to ignore the work of the others.

A uniformed police sergeant got up from a table and came to the counter. He had a round easy face that made him look like some sort of entertainer.

"My name's Martens," Jake said. "You're holding my brother here."

"Oh yes. The Canadian."

"The people at the High Commission said I could see him once before I went back to Canada."

"I see. Just let me check on that."

He walked to the other end of the room and picked up a telephone. As he spoke, his face was turned away from Jake, and he spoke so softly that Jake could only hear a murmur of sound. He hung up the phone.

"Seems we can manage it for you. Would you like to come along with me?" He came around the counter and led Jake down a short hallway, stopped and opened the door of a small room with several wooden chairs and a table. There was no window in the room and the ceiling seemed low.

Once again he wondered what he should say. He wanted to ask everything and yet to say nothing. As if someone had offered you the chance to talk to a dead man. You'd never know what to ask first. Jake realized suddenly that in their whole lives, he and John had practically never been alone together. When they'd met, Margaret or their mother had always been present. He wondered if he should tell John about the meetings with funny-eyes. But maybe the room was bugged. When he thought about it, Jake doubted if they'd be left alone.

There was a sound of voices in the hall and the door opened. Jake turned and looked. He saw John coming in with a uniformed policeman behind him. The policeman closed the door and went and sat in a chair at the far end of the room. John had walked up to the table and sat down without looking at Jake.

"Haven't seen you for a long time," Jake said.

"Two years, I think." He still didn't look up.

"A lot can happen," Jake said.

"You do understand that." He glanced toward Jake for a second, then looked away.

"In a way," Jake said.

"Margaret said mother asked you to come to England."

"Yeah, she was pretty upset."

"Does she know where I am now?"

"I phoned her when we heard."

"I'll write her a letter soon. That would be the best thing to do. To write to her."

There was a moment's silence. Jake looked at the

177

cop at the other end of the room. He was studying the cracks in the wall.

"How do you feel about the whole thing now?" Jake said.

"Very calm now. Everything is very clear and quiet."

"I don't know what you mean."

"It's hard to explain. It would take a long time to make it comprehensible to you. I think I may write a book about it. To make it all clear."

"Why did you do it?" Jake said. And why didn't I? he wondered.

"One must fight fire with fire," John said. "Also, it was a matter of circumstance. We make our history, but we don't make it just as we please. It's Marx who says that."

"He says a lot of good things."

"Being the man I was, at that moment, the choice was obvious. I had to step into history however I could, without scruples. You see, it's like a fire. You're either in or out."

Jake looked at his brother, at the way he almost pursed his lips after he finished speaking, and he wanted to shout at him that he didn't know what he was talking about. If you didn't listen, it made sense, but as soon as you listened carefully, it didn't reach you, suddenly seemed to fade out or disappear back into John's head. Was it just the circumstances of this visit, this room? Or was it more than that? What made John's words go dead in the air?

"I'm still not sure I understand," Jake said. He wanted John to look at him.

John looked down at the table and said nothing. Jake felt himself getting nervous and angry as the silence stretched out, nothing happening, no contact.

"I don't know what you're talking about," Jake said, suddenly feeling all the anger and frustration loosening

178

in him, "and I don't think you know what you're talking about."

John looked at him now. Directly at him, the eyes behind the glasses troubled.

"Why did you say that?" John said. "You're my brother. I've never done you any harm. You're just like all of them. It's all just a silly game because no-one is ever allowed to say anything .... You don't know what I'm talking about because no-one knows what I'm talking about. They come to me with their foolish questions, their little bits of information from my journals, and they expect me to play their game with them. The game of sides. Your side, my side. 'Why don't you tell us the truth?' they say. And I can only say that I can't tell the truth because they'd never know the truth. Never."

His voice was becoming shrill. He was almost screaming, and the policeman at the other end of the room seemed about to move toward him.

He began to speak again, his voice lower, but still strained.

"My journals mean so much to them, but they're just a story I made up, and I could have made up a dozen others. None of them would be the right story, none would be the story that could lead me to the ending I need. There isn't any story to lead there. You're too young to know that, to know the pain of almost remembering that once there was a story in your mind .... They're all such fools, you and all of them. But I don't care any more. All I want is to go to their jail because I'll be free there. They never understood, none of them, what I was doing. But someday everyone .... " He was starting to scream again.

"I'm sick of people asking for the truth ... suffering is the truth. No-one's allowed to say ... I've done something worthwhile because I did it. How could

179

you understand? I don't know you. You say you're my brother, but I don't know you."

He stood up. Jake stood too, not sure why, but feeling that he must stay face to face with him. The cop was moving up from the other end of the room.

"Someday people will understand," John said. "Someone . . . a few people will understand."

The policeman took him by the arm. John looked startled and terrified.

"Let go of him," Jake said.

The cop didn't move or react, just held John by the arm.

Jake felt a sudden impulse to touch him. Reached across the small table to take his two hands. He stood there, holding John's hands and facing him, and after a few seconds everything in the room seemed to grow still and calm. Jake dropped John's hands and sat down. The policeman guided John into his chair and moved back a couple of feet.

"I'm sorry," Jake said. "I guess I don't understand."

John looked at him for a long time before he spoke.

"Will you be in to see me again?" he said.

"Maybe," Jake said. "I'll tell Margaret and she can let you know."

He stood up. John and the cop stood up. John held out his hand, and Jake took it. He shook the hand and turned to go out. The policeman opened the door for him, and Jake walked through the police station and back to the street. He walked without looking, without thinking.

Walked. Walked.

He'd promised to see Lucy after the interview. Until now he'd put off planning his return, but now he had to settle everything.

He dodged a barrow loaded with crates of apples and turned the corner toward the tube station. He couldn't get over the feeling that all the activity he saw around

180

him, men working and talking, was unreal. Or that he was unreal, invisible.

He went down the elevator to the tube and set off for Lucy's place. Jake didn't like the tube at the best of times. Everyone sat in silent isolation, as if they'd turned something off when they got in and wouldn't turn it on again until they left the train. Except that today he found himself wondering if it would ever turn back on again. Maybe they were zombies, something left over from a failed experiment. Or names invented to pad a voter's list.

Jake tried to shake himself out of it. Since the talk with John he'd lost his hold on something. It was bad, the whole scene was bad. He wouldn't go back and see John again. There was no point in it.

Jake changed trains and rode on, remembering his brother talking quietly as they sat at the wooden table.

Jake took out his red notebook and a pen and began to write without thinking, just letting the words come on their own.

> There was a man
> Who shut his eyes,
> Shut his ears,
> Shut his head.
>
> He was a bad man.
> He was a dead man.
> Kill him again.

He closed the notebook and put it away.

Jake thought now he only wanted to get back, to talk to Member and the others, to get something moving. He wondered again about the prison, about deliberately getting sent in there and starting a movement inside.

He got off the train, went up the stairs and began to walk, walking fast so he didn't have to think.

When he reached the basement room, he knocked

on the door and waited. It was starting to rain, and he wondered what to do if there was no-one home.

Lucy opened the door.

"Hi," she said. "C'mon in." She looked nervous. She knew where Jake had been.

"Where's Hattersley?"

"He's down at the squatters' place again."

"How are they doing?"

"There's a lot of noise, but they're still in."

"Shit, that's good. That's really good."

"You look kind of freaked out."

"I saw my brother this afternoon."

"They really let you see him, eh?"

"Yeah."

"Did he say anything interesting?"

"Jesus, he said a lot, but I don't think he was talking to me."

"What's that mean?"

"I don't know. I really don't."

Lucy walked over to the chair where he was sitting and knelt on the floor beside him. She reached up to his face and kissed him.

"You'll be going back now," she said.

He nodded.

"Are you going to take me back with you?"

Jake waited a few seconds before he spoke.

"You once said you were tired of the revolution," he said.

"I'm tired of his revolution."

"It's all the same revolution, Lucy. Don's and mine are just the same. You wouldn't be any better off with me."

She got up and walked to the other side of the room.

"So you're leaving me here."

"You don't have to stay. You've got a ticket."

She didn't say anything.

"You can leave any time you want," Jake said. "And that's what you should do."

"Don't give me any advice, damn it. Just leave me alone."

She was starting to cry, and Jake was tempted to go across the room to her, but he told himself it would be foolish and turned toward the door. There were a lot of things he had to do.

Library of Congress Catalogue Card No. 77–157711
ISBN 0 88750 043 9 (hardcover)
ISBN 0 88750 044 7 (softcover)
Cover photograph by David Helwig
Printed in Hong Kong by Serasia Limited
PUBLISHED IN CANADA BY OBERON PRESS